A BANNER FOR PEGASUS

Also available in Perennial Libary
by John & Emery Bonett

DEAD LION

JOHN & EMERY
BONETT

★

A Banner
for
Pegasus

PERENNIAL LIBRARY
Harper & Row, Publishers
New York, Cambridge, Philadelphia, San Francisco
London, Mexico City, São Paulo, Sydney

A hardcover edition of this book was originally published by Michael Joseph Ltd. in 1951. It is here reprinted by arrangement.

First PERENNIAL LIBRARY edition published 1982.

ISBN: 0-06-080554-4

82 83 84 85 86 10 9 8 7 6 5 4 3 2 1

For
BETTY

1

Are we all met?
Pat, pat; and here's a marvellous convenient place . . .

MIDSUMMER NIGHT'S DREAM

HAZEL FAIRWEATHER wished the man would stop talking to her. She had been alone in the carriage when he got in. He was shabby, with a dimple in his chin and a pronounced adam's apple in the middle of a long, thin neck. His face was youthfully pink between sparsely scattered single hairs, and his eye was wild. His monologue had been about the Government first, then religion, all in a steady monotone into which quite gratuitous pieces of information were slipped, such as the fact that Mrs. Amory said he could have a bath whenever he liked, and that he had double-jointed elbows, to which it seemed that no response she could make would be really adequate. Hazel had felt relieved as the carriage filled up, but she now realized that the people getting in, finding them in conversation, assumed them to be travelling together, which did nothing to ease her situation.

Hazel stood up and took her attaché case from the rack. She moved out into the corridor, where two men with luggage instantly collided with her. The compartment to the left was full, and so was the next, with someone already standing. From the tail of her eye she observed that the madman, too, had left the compartment and was ambling in pursuit. Evidently he considered her a good listener. As Hazel went through into the next coach the train began to move. She pushed her way past several standing passengers, and presently the inspector pushed his way past her, pausing in his stride to clip tickets. When he was gone she realized she had missed her chance of mentioning that she was being molested, but in any case the inspector was too busy, and doubtless her pursuer had given her up or found another confidante.

There was clearly no sitting room, so Hazel put her case down and, leaning against a window, watched the little London back gardens scurrying by and worried about the washing. There was a child on a swing and another in a battered, soot-covered pram. Hazel stopped worrying about washing and worried about children. Something pressed against her arm and a grating voice in her ear said: 'There's a lot of rubbish on this train. Film trash on their way to the festival at Haddington. Mrs Amory didn't like the idea of my going on this train. Thought I might get carried on to Haddington with them. She doesn't know me.'

'Nor do I,' said Hazel, not very hopefully. 'Would you mind talking to someone else?'

'I'm not going to talk to any of that film trash,' protested the man cunningly. 'Not me. I'm too smart for that. Do you know what they want me for?'

Hazel couldn't guess. She was already moving into the next coach. This proved to be a first class coach, and here again the carriages were filled, though with only three a side in most cases. The occupants of the first two compartments were so much too well-dressed that Hazel realized they were probably some of the film trash already referred to that would remain on the train to Haddington when Hazel changed at Bratton for the branch line to Steeple Tottering. Hazel moved on down the corridor wishing she could encounter someone she knew, then, in the last compartment but one, she saw Mr. Hallam.

Mr. Hallam worked for the Catchment Board at Steeple Tottering, and had been her employer until she had moved across the road to the office of the *Sallowshire Guardian*. He was hardly the apple of her eye, but he was respectable and sane and he had the carriage to himself.

Hazel slid open the door, then slid it shut behind her. 'Hullo,' she said. 'Can I come in?'

'By all means,' said Mr. Hallam.

'I had a seat in a third class carriage, but a man kept talking to me. Someone a bit mad.'

'Well, if he comes in here we can pull the communication cord.'

'He's not really as mad as that. Can I sit by you?'

'Of course. It's a very warm day. I feel grateful that first class travel is one of the few luxuries I allow myself. The train is unusually crowded.'

'There are a lot of film people on it,' Hazel told him. 'Travelling up to the festival at Haddington. It's been going on all the week, but this evening the Western Counties Television station is going to open and the *Daily Trumpeter* has arranged to present a whole lot of Oscars or something during the inaugural programme.'

'Yes, to be sure,' said Mr. Hallam. 'I've been reading about it in my evening paper. Now let me see, it's Miss Fairbrass, isn't it? Left us a couple of months ago to go on the stage?'

'Well, actually, Fair*weather*,' said Hazel. 'And I went into the newspaper office across the road from your office. You see me almost every day.'

'Oh yes, of course. Did it work out more exciting?'

Hazel realized that his eyes were twinkling. 'Not entirely,' she admitted. 'But perhaps if I learn to do the job I've got really well, I shall get a better one.'

'Somewhere else?'

'I'll hardly make very much history in Steeple Tottering.'

'Don't you like Steeple Tottering?'

'Yes. I love it. It's beautiful. I was born there and I don't think I'll mind if I die there. But . . .'

'It's the time in between.'

'Sometimes I feel that I've got to escape.'

'You never escape that way, by going away from anywhere. I found that.'

'You did?' Hazel looked at Mr. Hallam attentively. 'Then how can you escape?'

'Inwards,' said Mr. Hallam. 'Into yourself.'

Hazel began to wonder if she hadn't overlooked Mr. Hallam, though he looked so exactly like every other

Civil Servant that she felt she could hardly be blamed for it. 'Wouldn't you have to have stored up a good deal of experience before you could do that?' she asked.

'I don't know,' he said, considering her question. 'Yes, possibly. But then one can experience things without them actually having to happen to one, surely?'

'By reading, you mean, or in imagination?'

'Oh, I think so. O yes, surely . . .'

Hazel would have liked him to go on but the train had stopped at Hawbridge Junction and people were pouring along the corridor in search of seats. The door was slid back and a porter came in with luggage, followed by a party of what was clearly more film trash, talking volubly and angrily about a mistake someone had made over the connection and the reservations.

The first into the compartment was a tall young man in corduroys with a green tie. He was followed by a hornet-faced woman wearing a skin-tight, dark-red sweater with a well-cut trouser suit, the jacket of which hung loose from her shoulders without her arms in the sleeves. She carried a portable typewriter which she wouldn't let the porter take, and seemed in charge of the arrangements.

'Only four seats in here,' she said brusquely. 'I shall need another two.'

Hazel pushed up the padded arm between her and Mr. Hallam and moved a little nearer to him. Her seat was in jeopardy. The padded arms still divided the opposite side into three enormous seats.

'Thought you had them all reserved, Murky,' said a

shortish, dark man coming into the carriage. He looked foreign, energetic and extremely consequential. 'Better get a move on and get something fixed up. We've got to talk. Can't waste the journey.' Two more people had crowded behind him into the carriage and there was another just outside.

'Plenty of room,' said the tall young man pleasantly, flipping up the two arms on the opposite seat. 'Mr. Porsen,' he bowed the foreign one into the corner opposite Hallam, 'Mercedes here beside you, Mr. Bertrand and Mr. Hollinshead.' He arranged the incoming couple in the other seats on the far side, then flipped up the remaining arm on Hazel's side. 'Gussie in the corner and me here.' He sat down between Gussie and Hazel, giving Hazel the faintest smile, while his fingers closed just for a second over her hand and folded her gloved fingers round the ticket she had been holding. Hazel realized that she had been holding the ticket ever since she had met the inspector, and that it was a third class ticket, and that the young man had noticed it too. Her heart gave a small leap that could not be entirely accounted for by the risk of exposure, and she slipped the ticket into her bag.

'Well, that's that,' said the one they called Mr. Porsen. 'I only hope nothing's gone wrong the other end.'

'Joey's arranging it,' said Mercedes in a distrustful voice. 'He's meeting us with a hired car and the unit car, but you know what Joey is.'

'I thought he was improving,' said Porsen.

'Not when he's got lumbago,' said Mercedes on a

captious note. 'And he can get it for anything, even in this weather. I tell him if he can't be more dependable he ought to pack up. You must have efficiency.'

'Sure,' admitted Porsen. 'We've got to have that.'

'Well, you never will while you've got Joey.'

'Joey's all right,' said the young man in corduroy. 'He'll be there. Have you seen his little girl?'

'No, I haven't,' said Mercedes, who plainly did not want to.

'Has he got a kid?' asked Porsen with genuine interest.

'Lovely little girl of three. You'll love her.'

'I always love kids.'

'I'll bet she's cute and ought to be in pictures,' put in Mercedes a trifle viciously, watching her boss.

'Joey never said so,' said the quiet voice beside Hazel, which then determinedly changed the subject. 'How long have we got before Miss Brentbridge starts working?'

'Eliza,' said Mercedes, 'starts Wednesday.'

'Elizabeth, the virgin queen,' said Porsen, clearly intending a joke.

'*Is* she a virgin?' asked Mercedes, clearly not recognizing it and prepared to believe *anything* about another woman.

'Better ask her husband,' said Porsen.

'I'd sooner ask you, Lars.'

'What a friend, what a loyal worker,' said Lars Porsen, who was beginning to emerge in Hazel's eyes as a wag. 'Here's little Mercy I rescue from the gutter and look after like I would my own daughter and all she can do is to blacken my reputation in front of strangers. What'll they think?' He almost bridled at Hazel who recognized him as the type that is incapable of not playing up to any woman, plain or pretty, who happened to be in the vicinity. Feeling unequal to the giggle or blush that his expression demanded, she turned her eyes apologetically to the window and he had perforce to continue without encouragement. 'Eliza's never worked for me before. Ask me in a fortnight.'

This was unmistakably a joke and was greeted with suitable hilarity by Mr. Bertrand, Mr. Hollinshead, Gussie and Mercedes, and by no means least by Lars Porsen himself.

Hazel was familiar with Elizabeth Brentbridge as a name and as a face, both perhaps the largest in British pictures, which greeted her from screens and hoardings, advertisements and magazines, over and above the imitations which greeted her from behind every second counter in the country.

'Lizzie's all right,' said Gussie from his corner. 'I had her in "Tarnished Madonna" and "Liliom of Lady-well." She's just a sweet natural kid. Do you know,' he added, as one who drops a bomb full of candy kisses, 'she never puts a scrap of make-up on, off the set.'

'She's just a great tomboy at heart,' put in Bertrand, determined that Gussie should not be the only one to reveal familiarity with the lady.

'She's no fool, though,' said Hollinshead. 'I did all her special dialogue for "Silver Stallion." She wouldn't have anyone else, don't know why. Knows exactly what she wants and sees she gets it. I'll tell you something else you mightn't guess. That kid's got a brain. What do you suppose she kept on the set to relax over, throughout that picture? Einstein's "Theory of Relativity." '

'How long was the "Stallion" on the floor?' asked the young man next to Hazel innocently.

'Seven weeks.'

'She can't have been a very quick reader,' said Mercedes, making the point feet first, then adding, 'Were you on the "Stallion," Holly? I never saw your name on the credits.'

Hollinshead wriggled. 'No, there was a bit of a slip-up. Too many people on contract for credits already. I just came in at the end and did the job.'

'That's how it is in pictures,' said Bertrand. 'Don't we know.'

'Well, there's no trouble about credits in my pictures,' said Lars on a note that was only superficially jocular. 'I get them all.'

'That's what I like about working for you, Lars,' said Bertrand. 'We all know where we are.' His voice was equally, but only equally, jocular.

'You all get paid,' said the director. 'I do the work; I take the risks and I get the credit. Sometimes I like to talk my ideas over with one or other of you to get a reaction. Everyone needs a new angle on a thing they've worked and slept and eaten with day in day out. That's why I keep you guys tagging along, because you don't always agree with me. I can't do with "yes" men. Argument stimulates me. But *I* find the story and *I* get the treatment made, and *I* do the basic script. That's why Pegasus pictures have got unity. Any bit of trimming I get in the form of a fresh angle or a bit of dialogue is neither here nor there. And if anyone thinks differently I can do without them. And they can do without me.'

'Well, anyway, they can try,' chimed in Mercedes, but her voice was drowned under a nervous chorus of fervent agreement from the men who had been given to understand that they were not 'yes' men.

The man on Hazel's right uncrossed his long legs slowly and took out his pipe. 'Just a minute, Porsen,' he asked quietly. 'Does this mean you also keep your art director tagging along to provide fresh angles and stimulus for *your* original structures and sets?'

The director turned on him a dazzling smile of boyish frankness. 'Don't get things wrong, Paul. Art's a specialist job. You have to have training and architecture, perspective too. I know how I want a thing to look and you give it me. Of course you get the credit. You've got a contract, haven't you?'

'Yes,' said Paul. 'I fancy we've all got contracts.'

'Sure, sure you have,' smiled Porsen, oozing warmth and goodwill. 'And you're all satisfied with them. You haven't worked with me before, Paul, have you, or you'd know just how well we all get along—don't we?'

There was a chorus from the men who were not 'yes' men to the tune that Pegasus Pictures was one big happy family.

'Why when we had Miranda Hume on loan from B.P.A. for "Little Sister," ' said Mercedes, 'she cried right through the end-of-shooting party to think it was all over.'

'Perhaps she'd seen the "rough cut,"' suggested Bertrand roguishly.

Porsen smiled like a benevolent uncle. 'See what I mean?' He shrugged cheerfully. 'See how they all make fun of my work?' He was theoretically addressing Paul, but in fact, he was also appealing to Hazel, who he seemed to suspect was not entirely under his spell. Mercedes took a paper bag out of an attaché case.

'What you got there, Murky?' asked her employer.

'Peaches,' said Mercedes. 'Want one?'

'Thanks,' said Lars, holding out his hand.

There were two in the bag. He took one, tipped the second on to Mercedes' knee, twisted the corners of the bag and placed it jauntily on his head with the corners from ear to ear. 'Napoleon,' he announced, assuming a mock heroic position with one hand in the bosom of his coat. Then with a jerk of his head he brought down the bag, caught it, cupped his hand round the neck, blew into it and, with the other hand, burst it with a resounding bang.

'Just a crazy guy, but quite harmless,' he explained, shooting another look at Hazel. 'Just one of those scatter-brained chaps you read about making moving pictures.' He picked up the peach which was lying on his knee, and, on the point of eating it, changed his mind. 'Like a peach, youngster?' he asked, offering it to Hazel.

'No thank you, Mr. Porsen,' said Hazel. 'Thanks very much.'

The director looked gratified. 'You know me?'

'I heard someone call you Mr. Porsen. Of course I know *of* you. Most people do.'

'I suppose they do,' admitted Porsen. He groped for a cigar-case and offered it to Hallam, who declined. 'Cigarette, then?' suggested the director.

'No really. I scarcely smoke, thanks.'

'Just one for the occasion,' pressed Porsen, and by sheer force of personality compelled Mr. Hallam to take one. Lars then passed the case to Hazel who took one without argument. Lars leaned back and relaxed at last. They were all one happy family. He would never set eyes on Hallam or Hazel again in his life, but they were all on his side. Everything was cosy.

'You know this is going to be a new one for you, Gussie,' said Porsen. 'You've got to have a different camera technique from anything you've done before. No glamour.'

'If I'm going to try and photograph Liz Brentbridge with no glamour, she won't like it.'

'Yes, she will. She doesn't know what she likes till she sees what I can do with her. This picture will Make her.'

'I thought she was doing all right,' said Bertrand.

'Not only her—you—me—the whole lot of us. It's going to do something for the prestige of British pictures. Do you know the original this picture is based on has been lying in Mantobar's files ever since he bought it two years ago? Do you know what Mantobar said to me when I blew the dust off it and said I'd like to do it?'

Nobody had an idea.

'Told me we couldn't make it in England. Said the only hope was to send a unit out to Italy where you could get the real, peasant, down-to-earth atmosphere. What do you suppose I said? "Manti, you can't get nearer to earth than Lars Porsen. Me, why I am a peasant." He said, "Maybe, but you've been around and it shows in your work. You're a very valuable director of fast-moving comedy, but you think in terms of cheesecake and double-takes. It won't do for this." "Mant," I said, "will you listen? I think that way because it's the way the public likes it, with the stories I've handled so far. But with this story I'll make the public see it the way I want them to see it, and like it the way I want them to like it. I've got vision, don't you see, and this story is *pure*. It hits me where I live— and for why? Because I'm a peasant. And the way I see it, the way I handle it, it'll hit the public where it lives— because in the main—they're peasants too." And suddenly he seemed to catch fire from me and said, "Okay, Lars, go ahead and make it," and asked me who I wanted for the parts. So I plumped for Lizzie and Coram McCoram and he let me have them just like that.' He snapped his short, powerful fingers.

'Lizzie's been awfully typed on wicked women in her last few pictures,' said Hollinshead.

'Don't you worry. I'm going to give the public a new Elizabeth Brentbridge—the real Elizabeth Brentbridge. The woman under the dross.'

'Does she know?' asked Bertrand.

'Sure she does, Bert. She's growing her eyebrows and

cutting her fingernails. She's very co-operative. She knows it's the chance of a lifetime.'

'She's right,' said Bertrand. 'It's a beautiful story. When you first outlined it to me, Lars, I don't mind telling you I was moved.'

'I cried outright when he read me his treatment,' said Mercy.

'It's got something we don't often come across in our business. A kind of poetry . . .' said Hollinshead.

'Simplicity.' Lars produced the word like a conjuror bringing a rabbit out of a hat. 'And everybody that's read it feels the same. Stars, distributors, even all you riffraff around me, admit we're working on something different, eh, Paul?'

Hazel suspected he appealed to Paul because he was the one who had volunteered no encouragement. Paul leaned forward and tapped out his pipe against his heel. 'It's a beautiful story,' he said very softly. 'God grant we don't rub all the bloom off its wings.'

'That's how we all feel,' said Porsen after a moment's pause. 'And if we approach it in that spirit, I don't see how we can fail. I've got a feeling about it, here,' he tapped his vest, 'and I'm keeping the dialogue to the absolute minimum. This is the sort of theme that teaches you the value of silence—with a good background music, of course. I visualized something sort of all on one note, only haunting you know—thing you get on your mind and can't forget, but all the same you can't remember it properly. Not the usual sort of sound-track music, either. Just one instrument I thought . . .'

Inspiration illuminated Bertrand's face. 'Something like a zither?' he suggested. He, too, had been to the movies.

'Could be,' considered Lars. 'You might have something there. Or maybe not a zither exactly but something *like* it—only quite different.'

'How about a guitar?' offered Holly, 'or—I know—a harp. That's never been done.'

'Now a harp might just be what I have in mind,' said Lars recklessly. 'Sort of twangling under the natural sounds of birdsong and purling water . . . only I don't know,' he began to doubt, 'I've never *heard* a harp used just by itself for background. Wouldn't people get fed up with it?'

'People didn't get fed up with the zither.'

'No, we know that *now*. But a harp? I've never heard one used for a sound-track. If I'd heard it just once in some obscure picture—and it had come off . . .' he broke off undecidedly. 'Trouble is, in my position you have to know everything. But I've got the right man actually to *compose* the music. Chap that did the stuff in "The Heart Goes Home." '

'Mario Fideli,' said Mercedes. 'He did a lovely job in that.'

'Mind you,' said Lars, 'I know exactly what I want for the theme of the thing. Heard it on the wireless. *Da*, da da *da*, da da *da*, da, da, da, *ting*, ting-a-*ling*, ting-a-*ling*, da, da, da . . .'

' "Sheep may Safely Graze," ' said Bertrand. 'It's by Bach.' He supplied a few more bars.

'That's it,' agreed Porsen, delighted. 'That's the

21

thing I've got in mind. Different, of course, here and there, I shall tell him, just enough so we don't infringe anything, but that's the atmosphere exactly. That's what I'll tell him to do.'

'Perhaps he'll want to do something by Mario Fideli,' suggested Paul.

'Nonsense. Makes his job easier. I tell him what I want and he gives it me—if he's any good. Then there's no trouble. A film has to be one man's conception. They are children.' Lars leaned forward and smiled explanatorily into Hazel's face. 'I tell them. I have to tell them everything. This girl'—his face was alight with visionary fire—'this pure child of nature, with just one shaft of sunlight on her through the fir trees, stepping naked into the water and the music—harp maybe—playing *da*, da da *da*, da da, *da*.' He swayed his thick little body to the rhythm while his mobile hands indicated the body of the girl.

'Naked?' said Hollinshead.

'What else?' asked the director. 'How else do you see her?'

'Lizzie Brentbridge?' said Hollinshead.

'Don't give me Lizzie Brentbridge,' cried Porsen in the frenzy of creation. 'This girl is pure—a clear fountain of limpid water, lit from within by her own high strange fire of destiny—so—she could be bare. It's right. It's beautiful. It's *inevitable*.' During the almost religious hush that fell over the carriage, Lars Porsen bit deeply into his peach.

'O.K.,' said Bertrand at last. 'I think you've got something there. Should be wonderful.'

'It's worth trying,' admitted Hollinshead, equally reverent. 'Even if it's risky.'

'Risky?' Porsen thumped his chest with the free hand. 'I *take* the risk. I know what I'm doing.'

'And Lizzie?' asked Hollinshead. 'Will she . . .?'

'Never mind Lizzie,' put in Gussie. 'She'll like it.'

'Then everyone likes it,' said Paul, and Lars said, 'Sure.'

But Hazel felt sure that Paul meant everyone liked it too much for him to like it at all. She longed to turn her head and look at this young man who seemed to say just enough to make her feel he was thinking exactly what she was thinking, that, in fact, they two shared an island in the middle of an alien sea. There was no question at all that everyone else in the unit was in total accord with everything their director said or felt, and that any opposition they at any point raised was done more to give him an opportunity of knocking it down than for its intrinsic merit. The reactions of Orlando Hallam on her left, however, were a more unknown quantity. Hazel felt that he listened entranced but quite uncomprehending, as might an intelligent explorer, coming upon a colony of natives whose language and customs he did not understand, eager to be instructed and quite uncritical. Once or twice he had leaned forward as though to hazard a question, but always someone spoke and he leaned back again to listen. It occurred to her, too, that anyone who didn't actually speak their language might have been pardoned for assuming that their conversation was sparkling with original wit, judging from the expressions on their faces and their frequent laughter. It was clear that they were persuaded of this themselves, since from time to time Lars turned to her with that deprecating shrug which seemed to say, 'You must forgive us if we are brilliant and even shocking, for we are film people and altogether outside your sphere.'

Despite his overpowering conceit he was not a dislikeable person at all, she realized, for the warmth of his personality, his vitality, and above all his intense desire to be liked could not but endear him. It was impossible, too, not to watch him all the time. The vigour of his enthusiasms illuminated his mobile features and twinkled in his kind, dark, intelligent eyes. He talked with his whole body, and it occurred to her that no railway carriage, or room, or even desert would seem empty while he were in it. On the other hand, now, as he suddenly got to his feet and made his way into the corridor, the carriage seemed to relax into something like emptiness.

Hazel became more conscious of the young man on her right and was hard put not to look at him. She could see without actually turning the outline of the lean knee under its corduroy trouser, his feet in dark-brown suède shoes and the tweed sleeve of his coat. He had hard, purposeful fingers and she was sure that his hair was dark and not absolutely straight. The rest she could only fill in as a blur of charm and ease of manner and keen intelligence. Mercedes, who sat opposite Hazel and could have looked at him easily, was making no use at all of her opportunities. She had taken out some knitting the moment Lars' departure had relaxed them all and was bent over the needles. It was a man's sleeveless yellow pullover. Hazel felt it was inevitably destined for Lars. Mercedes was Lars' familiar, though plainly a harpy to everyone else. She was not an actress, Hazel decided, nor anybody's mistress. She might be his secretary, or a script or continuity girl. Hazel was aware that all these callings existed in the film business, though precisely what their functions were or whether they could overlap she did not know. Mercedes was in her thirties with a reasonably good figure, but her eyebrows running upwards from the centre and two deepish grooves running downwards from nose to mouth produced two converging sets of lines which gave her a look of waspish ill-humour and alertness.

Bertrand had an amiable face, straight, thinning hair and the slightly harassed air of a family man. Hazel could not guess at his function, but Hollinshead in the far corner was obviously, from the conversation, some sort of script-writer. He had light hair and eyes and a somewhat timid manner, though his face, whenever he was addressed, sprang into lines of great eagerness. Gussie, in the corner opposite him, directly past Paul, could not be satisfactorily studied, but it was clear that he was the cameraman to whom was to be entrusted the religious rite of photographing Elizabeth Brentbridge—Bare.

Presently the train would stop at Bratton and Hazel and Mr. Hallam would change to the branch line for Steeple Tottering, leaving these people to proceed to Haddington in time for dinner and then the film festival.

25

Hazel wished she could know a little more about them before they vanished utterly from her life; about the picture on which they were shortly to embark and, more especially, what was the second half of the name of which the first half was unmistakably Paul; but she had not the strength of purpose to break the silence which, apart from the clicking of Mercedes' needles, had enveloped the carriage on Lars' departure.

Bertrand suddenly put down his newspaper and stretched his legs. 'You know the thing I like about Lars apart from his commonness,' he said comfortably . . .

The silence became absolute. Mercedes' needles had stopped clicking.

'Is his absolute refusal to regard anything as impossible,' finished Bertrand on a note of enthusiasm which contrasted strangely with his opening words.

They can't run him down even when he isn't there, because Mercedes will tell him what they've said, Hazel realized. Only, just for a moment, Bertrand had forgotten.

Lars made his entrance into the carriage and everyone drew back their legs to give him gangway. Alert expressions snapped back on to their faces.

'The weather doesn't look like breaking, anyway,' said Lars, 'for a good thing.'

'You can't count on it,' said Gussie. 'Why didn't you settle for Italy while you had the chance.'

'Because it's an English story,' said Lars, 'and it really happened. I'm going to photograph it where it happened. Besides,' he added on a matter-of-fact note, 'I never said I did have the chance to do it in Italy.

Three weeks will cover the location stuff and after that we go into Chiddingfield Studios. We've got six or seven weeks' intensive studio work, and even if we could do it in Italy, which as you very well know we can't, Eliza wouldn't go to Italy at the moment.'

'Couldn't we have found a new star over there? You could make an unknown girl in a part like that,' said Bertrand.

'With an accent that would either sound phoney or make everything else in the picture seem phoney? No, brother. I'm playing my hunch over the story. I'll play safe over the casting and stick to names. You can't force the public too far outside its groove.'

'So you don't think she's necessarily ideal for the part?' asked Bertrand.

'No actress is ideal for any part,' said Lars, 'unless the director can handle her. The public will come to see the Brentbridge and the rest is up to me.' He paused a moment, thinking, then added, as though his thoughts had surprised him, 'There's only one actress I can think of that would have been ideal for it—ten—fifteen years ago—and that's my wife.'

Hazel had the impression that the muscles under the corduroy grew tense beside her.

'Angela Wingless?' said Gussie. 'I didn't think she ever set foot outside the theatre.'

'That's right,' agreed Lars, 'but she had the quality born in her that I've got to force into the Brentbridge with my bare hands.'

'Ever thought of testing her?' asked Bertrand.

'Test Angela—for this?' cried Porsen hilariously.

27

'You think I'm raving mad? Have you ever seen her stripped?'

Hazel heard a sharp intake of breath whistle between Paul's teeth.

'Never,' said Bertrand, 'and I don't mean for this. Even fifteen years ago her features wouldn't have been regular enough. I meant for anything. After all, she's a magnificent stage artist. Hasn't she ever been tested?'

'Oh, sure, she made some early British pictures, now you mention it. Came out a bit like a camel. That was long before we were married. She says she'll never make any more. You know how she is.'

'But that was before films learned to handle artists whose features weren't as regular as sugar flowers on a wedding cake,' persisted Bertrand. 'We've come a long way since then. We know how to make use of brilliance like Angela's. I don't mean in juveniles or even leads, but dear knows we've got few enough genuine actresses —we ought to be able to find a place for her. Why don't you talk to Mantobar?'

'Not me,' said Lars Porsen. 'Angela's happy playing stage parts and I'm happy directing pictures. What could I do for her if I got her into a picture? To direct a woman she's got to have appeal for you, or, anyhow, mystery. You've got to feel there might be something coming your way, and that if it did it would be wonderful. There's got to be an adventure in it.'

'Husbands *do* direct their wives in some pictures,' said Hollinshead moderately.

'They're generally someone else's wife first,' said Lars. 'No. Give me a nice ambitious little artist like

Elizabeth to stimulate me and I'll have a masterpiece
in the bag before you know where you are.'

'Angela Wingless could act Elizabeth Brentbridge
and a dozen like her off any stage in the kingdom.' It
was Hazel's voice, creaking and breathless from long
disuse, exploding into the carriage like a hand-grenade.
In the ensuing hush, while she felt her whole face and
body growing hot, Paul's fist came to rest on her knee
with a slight, reassuring pressure and Paul's voice said,
'And when Elizabeth's wooden little face needs lifting,
Angela Wingless will still be able to command an
audience even with the back of her head.'

'Ah, an audience, maybe,' agreed Lars without
rancour. 'It's in a double bed that you feel the draught.'

This time the laughter was shrill but a little forced.
Lars wheeled back upon Hazel. 'But you know my wife,
do you?' he asked in a pleased voice. 'You admire her
as an artist?'

'Of course I do,' said Hazel, growing hotter in the
self-induced blaze of publicity. 'So does everyone, I
should think, who's seen her do anything.'

'That's right,' agreed Lars, watching her with close
attention. 'That's the way it is with people who admire
Angela. It's queer,' he appealed to the others, 'there
aren't any Angela Wingless fan clubs. She practically
never gets into gossip columns; her publicity photographs need a week's work, faking, before they're fit to
be used and ninety-nine out of a hundred youngsters of
to-day wouldn't know who she is. But the hundredth,
when you run into her, would go to the gallows blind-
fold for her like they wouldn't for Lizzie or Frank

Sinatra or possibly even Danny. And I know her. I've been to bed with her. I know everything she's likely to do or say from morn to midnight and back again to morn, and I can't see it. What's she got?'

The knuckles beside Hazel whitened but the voice came low. 'If you don't know, what's the good of anybody telling you?' Paul's face was dark red and at last Hazel turned to look at it and, in that instant when their eyes met, united in a lost cause, Hazel's heart took such a jolt as it had never experienced in its twenty-two years.

'O damn!' said Mercedes. 'You've made me drop a stitch.'

'Where?' asked Porsen, glad of a change from the subject that seemed to be diminishing his universal popularity. 'Here, let me see. I'll put it right for you.' He took the knitting and let Mercedes arrange the wool and needles in his stubby fingers. 'What do I do now?' She manipulated the wool in such a way that he took a blundering stitch.

'I can do it,' said Porsen. 'You watch me.' Peering and jabbing he managed to bungle through several stitches with a pinched-up, comic expression on his face that called forth a great deal of merriment, then, spurred on by his public, he put the knitting on his head, folded his arms in imitation of Queen Victoria and said, 'We are not amused.'

Whistling, the train tore through a smallish station. 'Belfairs,' said Mercedes. 'The next will be Bratton Junction where we change.'

'Change?' Lars tore the knitting from his head and

tossed it into her lap. 'You're not telling me we change again before we get there?'

'I've told you already,' said Mercedes, contentedly unravelling the last row of her knitting and beginning to undo the havoc that her lord had wrought. 'Nobody on God's earth, not even you, can put Steeple Tottering on the main line to anywhere.'

'Steeple Tottering? But aren't you going through to the festival at Haddington?' asked Hazel incredulously.

'Why should I?' asked Lars. 'Nobody's hanging any Oscars on me so far as I know. I'm going to Steeple Tottering to make a picture.'

'But—but why? I mean is there anything special about Steeple Tottering?'

'There is,' said Lars, and whether he would have told her any more, Hazel wasn't sure, for Paul's voice took over:

'A little outside the town there's a small spring in a natural basin called Wimpley Water. It has been untouched since the early part of last century, and there, eleven hundred years ago, legend tells of a little English shepherdess called Petronella who performed miracles. We're going to make her story.'

'How did you know—how did anyone know—about the legend?' asked Hazel.

'A man who lived locally investigated the whole thing and, over a period of years, sifted the facts and finally his findings were published in an extraordinarily charming little book two years ago. The film rights were bought through an agency by Simon Mantobar, one of the Pegasus producers. Fictitious names had been

31

substituted for the place names, but at the time of the purchase the author was persuaded to divulge them, and they were filed with the book and then forgotten.'

'And that's where Uncle Porsen found it, thick with dust, and recognized it for a natural,' cut in Lars, who could no longer be excluded from a story which did him so much credit. 'And I got cracking. During the last few weeks some of my unit have made a thorough survey of the places where it all happened, and they find them to be still untouched and pretty nearly perfect.'

'What was the book called?' asked Hazel.

' "Petronella," by Sidney Tremayne,' said Mercedes. 'It's a lovely story. A natural.'

'Of course, Sidney Tremayne is a *nom de plume*. You've got the real name there, Mercy, haven't you?'

Mercedes reached for her attaché case, but before she could open it Mr. Hallam leaned forward. 'You really needn't trouble to look it up, Mr. Porsen,' he said with a mixture of pride and humility. 'The name is Orlando P. Hallam, very much at your service.'

His face was alight with a smile of total happiness.

2

IN eight weeks on the *Sallowshire Guardian* Hazel had
learned certain things among which was the difference between her idea of news and Mr. Lightbody's.
Mr. Lightbody was the Editor, and, judging from the
eagerness with which his weekly paper was locally
consumed, Mr. Lightbody was right. To Mr. Lightbody's public the bursting of an atom bomb in Moscow
was not news in anything like the same sense that the
bursting of a whitlow in Steeple Tottering would be.
Bernard Shaw producing a new play at ninety-three
had absolutely nothing on Mrs. Appleby knitting a
hot-water-bottle cover at a hundred and one. In short,
Mr. Lightbody was a realist, while Hazel was a
visionary and it had to be admitted that every man,
woman and child in Sallowshire read his paper with
avidity and would have considered Friday a poor
occasion without it.

Hazel had recognized during her first fortnight that

her chances of becoming an ace girl reporter were slight. Her work had consisted of copying the names of prize-winning rabbits and poultry, along with those of their owners, in the local shows. In her third week she had risen to 'covering' the police court, and by the end of her second month she had attended and written up a school sports day, two school prize-givings, an agricultural meeting at the County Hall on the subject of abortion in cattle and another on artificial insemination —also in cattle—an old age pensioners' annual jamboree, twenty-seven funerals and forty-three weddings.

The practical things she had chiefly learned were the use of semi-colons and how to avoid starting a paragraph with 'The wedding—or funeral—took place' more than twice in the same issue.

There were, of course, more imaginative sections of the paper into which she had not yet been allowed to penetrate. There was the 'Young Folks' Column,' mostly syndicated material, 'Musings' (by Thinker), which had a determined flavour of uplift, 'In the Villages,' and 'Sallowshire Jottings.' In the last two all sorts of fascinating matters were discussed, such as quantities of salvage collected by boy scouts or amounts of fruit bottled by the W.V.S. in a given locality. Anything to do with foot-and-mouth disease got a headline to itself, and so, of course, did rape and arson; while murder would naturally qualify for a 'banner' or full-page headline, but so far, Hazel, though with the best will in the world, had not succeeded in stumbling on any such items. Everything that she had proudly brought in as news had been dismissed as of no local interest or reduced to a couple of lines in the 'Jottings.' Now at last and quite definitely she had got some news.

The question that exercised her mind while she typed some Council findings on local drainage was how she should tell it to Mr. Lightbody so that it also looked like news to him. Hazel scratched out 'urgent' and inserted 'imperative,' and thought deeply. Maisie, the second girl at present in the office, was similarly engaged on funeral reports, only by hand, Hazel having got the typewriter first.

Mr. Lightbody, who had been on the telephone in his office, put his head round the door.

'Good morning, Mr. Lightbody,' said Hazel. 'I've got something . . .'

'Oh, yes, Hazel,' he said cheerfully. 'Pop across to Mrs. Henderson's cottage at Sallow Bottom and find out which of her boys was run over this morning.'

Hazel's heart turned sick. She took a sharp breath. 'But—couldn't I find out from someone else?' she implored with a weakness quite unsuitable to her calling.

'Only take you a minute on the bicycle,' said Lightbody reasonably and not unkindly. 'It was at the level-crossing first thing this morning. Just find out if it was Philip or Ernest. Oh, and you might ask if they're putting in any claim against the railway. That's the third accident there in six weeks. Might give us a line, "Is this Corner of Sallowshire Becoming Death Trap for our Children," or something. Run along.'

'Yes, Mr. Lightbody.' Hazel got unhappily to her

feet, but Maisie, within an ace of getting the type-writer, behaved superbly. 'It was Ernest, Mr. Light-body,' she said. 'I met Philip on his way to school this morning. Ernest was seven last birthday, and his mother hasn't made up her mind whether to claim or not,' she finished hastily.

'Oh, good,' said Mr. Lightbody.

'Have the typewriter,' said Hazel, ripping out her unfinished story and pushing it across the table with a silent prayer of gratitude. Mr. Lightbody turned back into his room.

'Oh, Mr. Lightbody,' said Hazel.

'That's all right. Don't bother to go, Hazel. That's all for the moment. . . . Oh, unless you run over to Sam Wormwell at Littledown Farm and find out about his chickens being stolen. There's not much in it, but we're a bit short of "Jottings." '

'Yes, Mr. Lightbody. Would—do you—have you ever heard of Elizabeth Brentbridge?'

He turned back again in the doorway, kindly but impatient. 'Yes, yes, the name means something. Didn't she win the Western Counties Dairy Show Championship for quantity and quality of milk yield last year?'

Maisie made an explosive sound, then sat growing nervously but silently purple. 'She's a film actress,' said Hazel. 'I've got a story about her . . .'

'If she'd been a cow we could have used it,' said the editor, adding slowly and clearly, 'Dairy cows with local owners are local news. Film actresses aren't.'

'This *is* news,' protested Hazel. 'Lars Porsen—you

must have heard his name. He's married to Angela Wingless—is going to make a picture . . .'

'Whether I've heard of them or not they're not local names and their doings don't concern local people. When you've learned that you can begin to think you know something about local journalism. You'd better get over to Littledown right away.'

At Littledown Farm a pretty, slatternly girl opened the door and told her that 'Dad be down to the "Ring o' Bells" talking to a chap that wants to borrow his sheep.'

Hazel coasted downhill on her bicycle and parked it outside the 'Ring o' Bells.' Inside she ordered a tonic water and asked the barman if he would mind pointing out Sam Wormwell. 'Over there, Miss, talking to that foreigner,' she was told.

Hazel moved with her drink to a seat at the back of the settle where the two men were talking, intending to waylay the sheep farmer as soon as their conversation was done. Their voices reached her, but she was paying no attention to them until she heard the rich, Sallow-shire burr, easily identifiable as the farmer's, saying, 'Thirty-six sheep, clean and toidy for aafter the miracle baint the praablem; 'tis they dirty and decrepit ones you spoke on, for before, that I'll be hard put to find.'

'Oh, I feel sure we shall manage something,' the smooth voice of the 'foreigner' demurred. 'After all, most sheep get a bit grubby and used-looking by this time of the year. I think if we just picked out the thinnest of those you showed me for "before," and sprayed the bigger ones with a harmless white solution, we'd get the effect all right, if you're agreeable.' The conversation wandered on a little, then Hazel heard the word 'remuneration.' After this had been explained in simpler terms she heard Wormwell reply, 'No, Mister. So long as no harm be come to the sheep by the finish, I don't make no charge. When Joseph Gerridge lent some churns to the summer theatre that performed in St. John's Hall last year they didn't pay him no money, but they put a note, thanking him, in their programmes and gave him a paass for the rest of the season. Now I was thinking, suppose you do something like that, that'd be all I'd want.'

'But you don't understand. There won't be a programme. . . . This isn't a stage performance . . .'

'No, no. I understand that. But I seen it sometimes, on the screen at the start. Well, just put "sheep supplied by Sam Wormwell of Littledown"—oh, yes, and it would be best if you could just say how all my sheep were clean to begin with but some had to be dirtied, special for the first part—and then it won't cost you nothing.'

Hazel heard a slow, despairing expulsion of breath from the 'foreigner.' 'Simmering saints,' said the voice at last. 'So *you* want a credit title? Just as though there weren't enough people already falling over one another to get credit titles, now even the sheep expect them. Now, listen to reason, Mr. Wormwell . . .' the voice grew soft, reasonable, pleading. 'Fame isn't anything. Cash in hand is the only thing that matters in this world. . . .'

The persuasive voice faded in Hazel's mind to give

place to a sudden, dazzling arrangement of black capital letters: 'LOCAL SHEEP MAKE PICTURE.'

Her story was 'news' at last.

But when Hazel returned to her office, Mr. Lightbody was out. 'He's on to a wonderful story,' Maisie told her. 'Your Mr. Hallam of the Catchment Board has written a book and it's going to be made into a picture. He's gone across to interview him.'

'He would have,' said Hazel dispiritedly.

'Not that he's likely to,' added Maisie. 'I was at the window and saw Mr. Hallam going up towards the post office two minutes before.'

'Didn't you tell him?'

'No. I wanted to eat my sausage roll in peace. He came out from opposite almost at once, and he didn't come back. I suppose he's trying to find him in the town. Beasley's gone to lunch. Are you coming?'

'How can I?' asked Hazel. 'Someone's got to be here in case the Sallow gets on fire. The Thames wouldn't matter.'

'Ruby's in the front office.'

'That doesn't count. She's not reporting staff. I'll stay till someone gets back.'

She began to cheer up. Perhaps, after all, local sheep were better than a local author. In any case, as it happened, she was vouchsafed both, for Ruby, it seemed, had gone out for a moment. In a little while, hearing a deprecating cough in the front office, Hazel opened the intervening door to find Hallam standing beyond the counter with a slip of paper in his hand.

'Oh, hullo, Hazel. I just wanted to insert a small advertisement—a box number. I'm going to sell my bicycle.'

Hazel counted the words, took his money and gave him his change and his receipt; then she asked if he had met Mr. Lightbody. He had not. He was hers legitimately. She led him into her office.

Mr. Hallam was a little reticent at first, but when Hazel pointed out that the paper would print the story anyway, he agreed that in that case they might as well get it right. Hazel deftly extracted from him the facts that he was single, fifty-nine, and had at one time hoped to become a doctor, but had given it up on his father's death in order to earn a living as the most insignificant member of the staff in the office where he now held a job of some responsibility. He had lived with his sister until she died a year ago, and now had a Mrs. Jewel come in to 'do' for him every day. His recreations were walking, reading and collecting stamps.

'You see,' he smiled suddenly, 'I've lived in the same house all my life and worked in the same office for forty-one years. My sister was never very strong, so I never dared to consider leaving a position that assured me of a pension. I couldn't have escaped outwards, could I?'

'So you escaped into Petronella,' said Hazel. 'And now I suppose she's made you independent if you choose?'

'Not altogether. The film company paid me two thousand pounds for the licence to make the moving picture, but nowadays such a sum, even invested, does not necessarily yield a living. Besides, though it is hard for one of your age to realize it, it is better for a man to have an office where his presence is required every day. So many people die before they need for want of being necessary to anything in the world.'

Hazel felt a chill breath of loneliness invade the office, though the sun still blazed through the dusty windows, and groped for some suitable reply.

'You may say,' continued Hallam, 'that if I were to die my desk would be filled quite adequately within a week. That may be true, but at least I need not know.'

'But Petronella,' said Hazel, having found the reply she sought for. 'Please tell me how you came to find out about her.'

His face lit up and the blight was gone from the air. 'Oddly enough it was my work for the Catchment Board that first brought me into contact with the story. An old crone filling her kettle in the Widdle which is the smallest tributary of the Sallow, told me there was no water like Wimpley Water spring and that, if the farmers knew how to make use of it, they'd soon put a stop to foot-and-mouth disease.'

'I wonder if they would?' said Hazel thoughtfully.

'I wonder. I daresay it would require an act of faith as well, and that's harder to come by nowadays. I asked her what she meant, and she said it was what her mother had told her and that she was long since dead. I inquired in the woman's village and learned a little more, and bit by bit, continually asking questions and often listening to rigmarole that led me nowhere, I pieced together the legend and wrote it down. You haven't read it, I suppose?'

'I'm going to buy it the first time I go into Bratton.'

'You won't get it. It's out of print now. . . . No, it didn't sell out or anything like that, but it was remaindered. I purchased several copies at the reduced price. I shall be happy to give you one.'

'I'd love that,' said Hazel. 'Did she really cure foot-and-mouth disease?'

'Not so far as we know. This was some plague that attacked the sheep. It swept the countryside and no one dared to eat them. An edict was published that all the sheep, sick or well, had to be burned, which threatened serious poverty in a sheep-farming area like this. Then someone heard that up in Pennyfold and Ashlington, in the low hills above Steeple Tottering, where the flocks were watered at the natural spring of Wimpley Water, the sheep did not suffer from the plague. Petronella, a young shepherdess who lived near the pool, bathed every day in Wimpley Water and, where she bathed, the infected sheep, drinking, were cured.'

'Pennyfold's my own village,' said Hazel, 'and I never knew.'

'It is natural to cry for wings,' replied Hallam, 'when it is eyes and ears we lack, and patience to be interested in little things—natural, anyway, when one is young—probably more just too. It leaves the little things to be discovered by those who are too old to fly and who must find adventure at their doorstep or not at all.'

'But go on,' said Hazel. 'Is there any more?'

Hallam smiled and linked his fingers across his neat,

dark-trousered knee. 'From far and near shepherds began to climb the hill with straggling flocks of halt and failing sheep which drank at the water and were cured. Some came with lambs so weak they had to be carried; and many, far too many, died on the way up. The townsfolk sent a petition. It was too hard. Petronella must come down to the town and bathe in Sallow Water, the big pool fed by the Sallow, which was the town's natural reservoir, so that all might be saved.'

'She came?'

'Of course, but she made one stipulation; at sunset the town must draw its curtains and everyone remain indoors till she had bathed and gone back to the hills.

'But a miserable craven creature, Peter the Poacher, hid himself in some rushes and stayed till the sun went down. He saw her come down to the water, alone, in her homespun clothing, looking neither to right nor left, so sure was she that no man would try to see her. And when she had stripped off everything, even her shift, instead of her naked body he saw only a dazzling light plunging into the water. The vision was so intense and terrible that he fainted. He recovered consciousness, however, in time to attend the banquet of roast mutton that was given to celebrate the curing of the sheep. There was much eating and drinking and merrymaking till at last, drunken, he forgot his terror and began to boast that he saw the body of the little saint plunge naked into the lake.'

'But he didn't.'

Hallam shrugged his shoulders. 'I believe that is frequently the case with men who boast. The townspeople were shocked and then afraid; the saints would be angry and would surely avenge it on the town. Taking it upon themselves to forestall any such action they put out the offending eyes of Peter the Poacher with hot irons and stoned him from the town.'

'What did the shepherdess say?'

'She didn't know.'

'Never?'

'Not till years later. The town prospered. The legend had grown around Petronella that God would punish with blindness anyone who saw her naked, and as she was still believed to bathe every day in Wimpley Water the children were afraid of her and dared not play near the spring, till one day a child, running away from her, stumbled and fell. She comforted him and asked why he was afraid and he told her about the man who had watched her long ago and the penalty he had paid. She was deeply distressed. She said: "But it was for their sakes, not mine, that I said they must not look, for fear they should not be able to bear the light. He has been made blind by man, not by God and not by me."

'Quite old now, she set out to find him and, at last, after years, came upon him, a beggar in misery and squalor. People warned her not to touch him or speak to him, but to leave him a little food and a coin and pass by, since he was a man made blind by God for an ancient sin. When she tried to rouse him from his squalor he did not know who she was. He said: "I am an outcast and accursed of God. Give me some money and let me be, lest it come upon you too."

'Then Petronella fell on her knees and put her arms

44

round him, saying, "There is no curse of God. We must go together and to every place where you have begged and have published this thing we must publish the truth, so that men may love their Maker and not fear Him."

'But Peter said, "Leave me alone. You are gentle but if you have any dealings with me you will have no luck."

' "I do not need luck," replied the shepherdess. "I have the grace of God and that is enough for two. Come with me and I will care for you and lend you the sight of my eyes."

'So they went at last, together, on an endless pilgrimage, through all the places where he had begged and defamed the name of the Lord, and the end of their story is lost in obscurity.'

In the silence that enveloped the two, the door swung open and Mr. Lightbody came in, looking hot and rather irritable.

'Hullo,' he said, then, seeing Hallam. 'Oh, good. I've been looking for you all over the town.'

'Hazel and I are old colleagues,' said Hallam, rising. 'I'm afraid I've been boring her with the story of my life.'

'Splendid,' said Lightbody, looking over Hazel's notes. 'You've got the essentials, have you? Born in Littledown—lived there all your life. Good. Now just some little touch of human interest to give it life . . .'

'I'm afraid I can't manage anything like that.'

'Oh yes, we'll find something. What did they say at home? They must be proud of you . . . oh no, of course. Your sister—yes, yes, last year.' Lightbody's face sobered suitably for the necessary fraction of a second, then broke into an encouraging smile. 'But there's someone, now, surely—to share your triumph—a nephew, come, a dog or a cat?'

But no, Mr. Hallam could offer nothing so accommodating, not even a Siamese cat, though he had seriously considered one of these.

'You should get one,' said Mr. Lightbody rather peremptorily. Hazel laid a hand on his sleeve.

'Mr. Wormwell's sheep have been engaged to appear in the picture,' she said very quietly, as though it might or might not be important, but she was no judge.

'Sheep?' Lightbody's face lit up. 'Sam Wormwell's sheep of Littledown Farm, going to be filmed.' He slapped his knee. 'Heavens, what a story. Oh, well, that's all then.' He turned to dismiss Orlando Hallam. 'I needn't trouble you for any more. Thanks very much.'

Orlando departed.

'Splendid,' said Lightbody. 'I'll pop out and have lunch while you copy your notes. Then I'll knock them into shape.' At the door he paused. 'Have you had your lunch?'

'Not yet,' said Hazel. 'Beasley must be back in a minute. I'll go then.'

Hazel wrote out her story, thinking gloomily the while on the inevitable punishment it must receive from her boss before he would consider that he had knocked it into shape. If the story had been of less importance it would have been subbed by Beasley who would have made only the minimum of alterations out of respect for

Hazel's feelings. Hazel respected Beasley's feelings in other ways, so the arrangement was mutual, if un-expressed. But Lightbody's gift, which had got him to the top, lay in never using one simple phrase where two clichés could serve and of course, he was right. Hazel had to admit that the paper would have been nothing without him. He could wrench human interest out of a timetable.

Beasley returned from his lunch wearing the expression of a permanently expectant father, and Hazel left for hers. There was nothing left at the China Dog, where she normally got two courses for one-and-nine, so she decided to bang three-and-sixpence at the 'George' and made her way to a small table in the corner. Looking up from her menu she saw that most of the Pegasus film unit lingered over coffee at the window table. Paul had his back towards her and Lars and Mercedes were missing. Dobell, the man she had seen in the 'Ring o' Bells' was there and another couple she hadn't seen before.

There was a great air of speaking freely and from time to time voices were dropped to criticize Lars or his methods. Dobell was telling them of his interview with Wormwell and a shout of laughter went up when he reached the point where the farmer had asked for a screen credit for his sheep.

'Of course, to be fair, they'll probably earn it,' said Bertrand judicially. 'I daresay they'll act the Brent-bridge off the screen.'

'That wouldn't be very difficult,' said Hollinshead, who, Hazel remembered, had been upholding her the day before when the wind blew from another quarter.

'It won't matter,' said Dobell. 'She'll look wonderful and the script's got everything.'

'That's right,' agreed Bertrand, flinging out an arm. 'And now,' he declaimed, 'the versatile star of "Tarnished Madonna," "Liliom of Ladywell," and "The Silver Stallion," portrayer of purity—wickedness—and split-personality (all on the one, slightly flat note provided by her Maker) in this, the greatest, strangest part ever written for a woman—Saint Petronella! *New* white heights of frigidity, *new* flats of diction, *new* wastes of desolation. If there is any emotion you have not seen this actress depict, you will not see it now. If there is anything you have prayed to be spared from seeing— *this is when she will do it.* Retained for a second week at the ENORMOUS Empyrean cinema.'

During his speech a vast and quite extraordinarily ugly man had made his way to Hazel's table and was now inquiring if the other seats were occupied. Hazel assured him they were not, and he sat down and regarded the menu. Presently he leaned forward. 'Pardon me, have you any experience of the "Poisson au Gratin"?' he asked courteously.

Hazel considered. 'I don't think it would be very advisable as it's Monday,' she replied. 'Especially "au gratin." You wouldn't be able to tell.'

'What a grasp you have of reality,' he said respectfully. 'The lamb cutlet, I fear, will inevitably be "off." I suppose I shall have to content myself with "cold buffet." '

'I expect so,' said Hazel. 'I did. The salad is beetroot and cold mashed potato, but the ham is really good.'

'Then cold buffet it shall be,' he said, and signalled his wants to the waiter, then turned back to her. 'My name is Mandrake,' he told her. 'And yours, I am convinced, is Persephone.'

Hazel told him her name and asked him if he were a celebrity. 'Do I look like a celebrity?' asked Mandrake, assuming a hurt expression, though actually rather pleased.

'On the whole, yes,' said Hazel. 'You see I'm a newspaper woman. It would be awful if you were a celebrity and I didn't find out. You're obviously a stranger here and I don't think you're one of the film team. Look, you started this, so if your name's a household word it's only fair that you should tell me.'

'I'm a professor of anthropology,' admitted Mandrake. 'And once in a way I get talking on the air.'

'That's it. I've seen your photograph in the *Radio Times*.'

'I've often thought that I might even get fan-mail if they didn't publish it so often,' said Mandrake wistfully, then he quickly added: 'I see I've left you with nothing comforting to answer. Please don't be distressed. Being hideous has its advantages.'

'Well, I've never been in the glamour class myself,' said Hazel. 'And nobody's ever asked me to go on the air. It looks to me as if you're doing all right.'

'You seem to be a kind girl,' said the professor. 'That's going to be a disadvantage in the newspaper world.'

Mercedes came into the room and moved briskly to the window table. 'Where's Lars?' she asked sharply. 'He said he'd made some dictaphone notes for me, but he's not in his room.'

'He's gone back to the hangar,' Bertrand answered. 'He doesn't like his room.'

'Why not? It's the best room.'

'It's a glorious room,' said Dobell, 'but it's exactly over the public bar and the darts team makes too much noise.'

'Why doesn't he change with someone.'

'Oh, we've all offered him our rooms,' wailed Dobell. 'We've insisted *ad nauseam*. But he just won't *hear* of it. He's being a *trouper* and roughing it with his men.'

'I suppose he took a car,' said Mercedes. 'Oh, damn, I don't know how we're supposed to get about across miles of country without a bit more transport. Joey's taken a car to the station to meet McCoram.'

'Have ours,' said Paul getting to his feet. 'I've decided to get a bicycle.'

'Just for three weeks? It's hardly worth it.'

'I'll get a second-hand one and sell it again when we finish. It'll be glorious coming down these hills.'

'Hellish going up them,' said Mercedes, then recalling upon which side her bread was buttered, 'Still, of course if you like it. Well, thanks awfully. I'll borrow it for now, anyway. Where are you going to get a second-hand bike?'

'Put a small advertisement in the local paper,' said Paul, moving towards the door.

Hazel demolished her blackcurrant roll in two bites,

collected her bill, said a polite but choked good-bye to
Mandrake, paid her bill, tore along the road and got
into the front office just as Paul was leaving.

'There's one on the spike,' she cried breathlessly.

'I beg your pardon . . . oh, good afternoon,' said
Paul.

'One what?' said Ruby.

'A bicycle. I took it while you were out. Mr. Hallam
just across the road wants to sell his. It'll save waiting
till our paper comes out on Friday.'

Paul regarded Hazel with a slow, pleased smile. 'You
really are invaluable,' he said.

He ,showed no surprise that she should know he
wanted a bicycle, or that she should happen to have
one on her at the time. Perhaps young women always
tumbled, breathless out of the blue, to offer this young
man what he wanted precisely when he wanted it.
Hazel felt it must inevitably be so.

'It's that top one, Ruby,' she said. 'Will you get it off
the spike?'

'We're not supposed to,' grumbled Ruby, doing so
and unfolding it. 'Look, it's a box number too. We're
not supposed to disclose the addresses of box numbers
to the customers, even after publication. They're a
sacred trust.'

'Somebody wants to sell a bicycle and somebody
wants to buy one. If he has to wait till we publish it'll
be too late to be much use. We're under no sacred trust
not to use our common-sense.'

'What about the receipt book?' said Ruby, using hers.

'Ruby is right. Put it back on the spike,' said Paul.

'We should all respect a sacred trust—especially when it's backed up by the receipt book. After all, I can get in touch with Mr. Hallam at my own risk. Did you say he was across the road?'

'He is if you go out through my office,' said Hazel.

'May I?'

Hazel led him across the passage. 'It's not my personal office, just "Junior Reporters." If I were you I wouldn't relinquish your share of the car altogether. I do quite a lot of bicycling around here. It isn't *all* downhill.'

He stood still in the doorway. 'Now how in the world do you come to know all about me? Even a junior reporter can't be so good as that.'

'I was in the "George" having lunch.'

'I never saw you . . . Why didn't you speak to me? Were you alone?'

'No. I was with a man.'

'A large man?'

'Yes.'

'I saw *him* all right. Is he a relation?'

'No, a total stranger.'

'A perfectly enormous, wicked old man comes and picks you up in the "George," so you won't speak to me.'

'I am speaking to you. He isn't wicked. He was nice and—rather wistful about his appearance.'

'He recognized you as a sympathetic type and tried to play on your feelings.'

'He didn't try anything. He was nice.'

'Don't you ever dislike people at sight?'

'No. Nor do you, I expect.'

He smiled. 'Not really. You're perfectly right.' But then his face sobered and his mouth became a short hard bitter line. 'Except one,' he added slowly. 'From the very first moment I met him I have loathed Lars Porsen like hell.'

The words fell oddly on the dusty, sunlit air. Paul shook his head and smiled shamefacedly. 'Now why in the world did I have to tell you that?'

'Don't feel depressed about it. People always tell me things.'

'It's the air of expectancy on your face. We don't want to disappoint it. It's disastrous.'

'I'm sorry.'

'At all events, I shan't tell you about my operation.'

'Have you had an operation? But then, ought you to ride a bicycle?' Hazel was genuinely concerned.

'Oh, that's all right. It was only for . . .' he stopped and regarded her suspiciously. 'You deadly woman. I shall go and call on Orlando before I start telling you my cute sayings as a child.'

Hazel watched him go regretfully. She could think of nothing more spellbinding than to hear his cute sayings as a child. She stood at the window as his tall figure crossed the road and entered the office opposite. She still did not know his name.

3

You meaner beauties of the night,
That poorly satisfy our eyes
More by your number than your light,
You common people of the skies,
What are you, when the Moon shall rise?

SIR HENRY WOTTON

B Y Wednesday the townsfolk had grown to some
extent accustomed to the invasion and even the
whitewashed sheep had ceased to occasion surprise when met at the turn of the lane. Elizabeth
Brentbridge was on the whole a disappointment,
appearing, except when made-up for her scenes, in a
jersey and a rather 'seated' flannel skirt, with a flawless
but actually rather shiny face, determined to be unaffected if it killed her, and spreading a good deal of
disillusionment thereby.

Coram McCoram, on the other hand, did try to live
up to requirements. He was six-foot-two and strikingly
good-looking in period or peasant clothing, though, it
had to be admitted, appalling in modern evening dress.
He had not been in pictures long enough to have
reached Elizabeth's degree of sophistication and conse-
quently broke into flamboyant colours on the slightest

provocation. He had a magnificent torso and wore his shirts deeply unbuttoned. He had reached stardom on the strength of two 'untamed' parts and one schizophrenic. Watching him, in action or repose, Steeple Tottering felt it was getting its money's worth.

Hazel had a choice of two roads to her work every morning; the quick way down past the Toad Rock and the longer, winding road which took her within sight of Wimpley Water. On the way home the longer road was a little the quicker, since the slopes were gentler and more easily negotiated on a bicycle. Early on Wednesday evening Hazel found Orlando Hallam leaning on the hump-backed bridge over the Wimple, gazing at the straggle of cameras, sheep and local children some couple of hundred yards away to the left. A coppice of shrubs and trees hid the actual Wimpley Water basin and provided shade for the sweating technicians and performers.

Hazel dismounted and greeted Mr. Hallam, who seemed eager to explain that his presence had nothing to do with the fact of his film being shot. 'One naturally does not wish to interfere in any way with the work in progress,' he protested. 'But, of course, it's very interesting.'

A number of unit cars were grouped beside the road, but, as no bicycle was visible, Hazel was able to devote her mind entirely to Orlando's problem. He was evidently aching to be in at the shooting and far too diffident to do anything about it.

A small car came up the road and stopped. Mercedes got out from behind the wheel, calling out as she crossed to the field-gate, 'Hullo. Have they got any-where in the last half hour?'

'I don't know,' said Hallam. 'We didn't care to intrude.'

'Then you're the only people in Steeple Tottering who didn't,' called Mercedes. 'Come along, they'll be packing up in half an hour.'

They followed her gratefully.

They found Lars in shirtsleeves, in his element, directing the sheep and the shepherds, keeping his head, keeping his sense of humour and keeping his temper with the sheep and the children who were under his feet all the time. Everyone sweated and shouted, or sweated, and was silent for a take, while, remote from it all, under its larches and silver birches, purled and bubbled the silver-tongued water that was the cause of it all.

'You can tell what a genius he is, now,' whispered Mercedes. 'Do you know he's not had a break except for coffee and sandwiches the whole of the day, and he's been at it like this since half-past eight? Everybody else has been asleep on their feet since two, but that man's a human dynamo if ever there was one.'

Lars was showing one of the actor shepherds how to step across the stepping-stones as nimbly as a ballet dancer, and Hazel recognized that what Mercedes said was true. Wormwell, the genuine shepherd, stood smoking a cigarette and looking singularly unreal against a group of actor-shepherds, whose make-up ran with sweat. Most of the company had found themselves places under the bushes out of the heat of the sun and a make-up man squatted with his trays of Max Factor under an ash tree.

Mercedes took her script back from Hollinshead and sat on a canvas chair in the thick of the battle. Hollinshead stood up and looked at Hazel and Hallam with an air of remembering the faces but not quite recalling the names.

'I expect Miss Brentbridge would like to meet Mr. Hallam and Miss er . . .'

'Fairweather,' said Hazel.

'She loves her part and she isn't doing anything just now,' went on Mercedes, prompting Hollinshead and eager to have them off her hands.

'O.K.,' agreed Hollinshead. 'Would you like to come over and meet her?' As they crossed the grass he added, 'You're sure to adore Liza. Not a scrap of affectation. Doesn't even use make-up off the set.'

Hazel was beginning to wonder if this mightn't be the greatest affectation of all, but Elizabeth's welcome was warm. She told Hallam that it must be wonderful to be an author and asked him how he thought of his ideas. While Hallam floundered through a reply, Hazel's eyes scoured the location for anything in corduroy trousers, but could find no sign of Paul. Elizabeth announced that it was really a privilege to play Petronella, and that she intended giving a party at the 'George' on the Saturday of the following week. She wanted Orlando to come, and Miss . . .'

'Fairweather,' said Hazel.

'Yes, of course, Miss Fairweather. Mr. Hallam did

say you were on the press, didn't he? You will manage to come, won't you?'

Elizabeth looked as though it was really very important indeed that Miss—er—Fairweather of the local press should come. It was quite a feat, and Hazel felt that she deserved her reputation as an actress after all.

Lars was in full cry again and twice shot Hazel a look which suggested he had no idea who she was and couldn't think what she was doing there. Hazel moved back to Mercedes, since, if it came to the point, she was there at her invitation.

'It's at times like this,' said Mercedes confidentially, 'that I'm glad my mother didn't turn me into an actress. Look at McCoram, battling to get his left profile used instead of his right. And look at the way Lars handles him. It's a treat to watch a brain like that in action. It's the onlookers who see most of the game.'

But Mercedes wasn't an onlooker either, thought Hazel. She was as much part of the game as any of them. Even bewildered, enchanted Orlando was warp or woof of this fantastic tapestry. Hazel was the onlooker.

And then as three men came back through the coppice she too ceased to be an onlooker or anything but a throbbing, vulnerable human organism, trying not to breathe too loudly or do anything whatsoever to draw attention to herself.

She succeeded. As Paul and Bertrand passed without stopping, Mercedes asked, in a confiding voice, 'Was the Brentbridge in a good mood?'

'Oh, I think so,' said Hazel. 'She asked us to a party.'

'She would. Sweetness—that's her thing. No affectation. No make-up even. I used to be in that line myself, but I can't compete. Now I use all the make-up I can lay my hands on.'

'Do you,' said Hazel rather nervously. 'Well, it suits you.'

'You could take a bit more, yourself,' went on Mercedes purposefully. 'If you don't mind my saying so, that's not your colour lipstick at all. What is it?'

'It's called Maidenbloom. I bought it because it seemed harmless.'

'That's just what it looks. You're not giving yourself a chance.' She regarded Hazel through half-shut eyes. 'Your colour is Caribbean Orchid,' she announced at last in the voice of a seer. 'Like to try?'

Mercedes plunged into her bag and after a struggle brought out an ornately encrusted gilt case and insisted on Hazel scraping off the Maidenbloom and replacing it with the luscious magenta of the Caribbean Orchid. 'It's marvellous,' she said. 'Does something for you, doesn't it? You can have it.'

'But . . .'

'I'm not using it. I brought it back from Paris, but my skin's too yellow. It brings out all the best tones in *your* skin. You like it, don't you?'

'Well—but . . .'

'Keep it.' There was no possibility of refusal. Almost as an afterthought she added, 'Cost me about fourteen shillings, but then the exchange was against me. You can have it for seven-and-sixpence. Don't bother to pay now. Any time will do. We're bound to see lots of each other.'

Hazel put the lipstick into her bag. Experience had to be paid for. Doubtless she had learned something in the last few moments which would prove cheap at seven-and-sixpence, but for the present she could not be sure. It was a quite good lipstick, anyway, and since it was certainly wrong for Mercedes' dark hair and swarthy skin, it might quite reasonably be right for her own more delicate colouring.

Mercedes gave a sudden, stifled ejaculation and, following her gaze, Hazel saw that Lars, who had completed the shot he had been working on, had approached a curly-headed girl and was tousling her hair and talking banteringly with her.

'Is she in the picture?' asked Hazel.

'Not so far,' said Mercedes between clenched teeth. 'Just a bit of local talent that's been trying to catch Lars' eye all the afternoon. She's the daughter of Wormwell, the shepherd whose sheep we're using. Lars is so good-natured anyone can make a fool of him. All over *you* that Sunday in the train, wasn't he? Next week it'll be me.'

Hazel recognized the girl now as the rather surly young woman she had spoken to when she went to find Wormwell, only much curlier and dressed in what was evidently her best dress. She sparkled back at the director, delighted to be the object of his raillery, until, clearly unable to endure any more of it, Mercedes got to her feet and moved across the grass to Lars.

'Mr. Hallam is here,' she told him, 'the author. You'd better speak to him.'

Lars took the child by the neckband as he might a puppy, and crossed the grass with her to welcome Orlando, who was charmed to be so greeted.

'There are just one or two points,' whispered the author, 'things that occurred to me. I wondered if you'd care to discuss . . . if you're not doing anything for a moment . . .'

'Of course, of course,' said Lars. 'I'd be delighted. Only not just now. This is the time, while my mind is active, that I like to spend up on the hilltop, alone with nature, wrestling with the problems of the coming day. Just for an hour. I refresh myself. I renew myself. Then I am ready for everything that can confront me. But to-morrow, another day, I'd be delighted to have a chat, any time you like.'

He squeezed Hallam's hand in dismissal. 'That's all for the day,' he boomed across the meadow to the rest of the unit. 'Come and see me to my car, darling,' he said to the girl in whose neckband his finger was still looped and, with a wave of his other hand to the rest of the unit, set off with the child across the grass. Wormwell looked after his daughter, then back at his sheep, then he decided to round up his sheep first.

Paul's shadow lay across Hazel's knees.

'Would you care to see me to my bicycle?' he said.

Hazel stood up without a word.

He led her in silence across the grass and back through the trees the way he had come. They came to the place where the stream widened and sunlight slanted down through the trees to strike the water in dazzling shafts.

'You will probably say you've seen the place a dozen times,' said Paul, 'but the fact of the matter is that I made it this afternoon with my bare hands. That shaft of light,' he pointed to the brightest beam that lit the sparkling water, 'wasn't there yesterday. I personally cut down three of the little branches at the top of that tree.' His finger traced the beam back to its source. 'The only thing that saddens Lars is that it isn't going to be in technicolor. Then we could have put in a couple of red and green jellies in the tree-top and had a stained-glass effect on the poor girl's torso as well.'

'Is it going to shine on Miss Brentbridge's torso?'

'Naturally. Of course we're shooting from over here, and by then we'll have thoughtfully arranged a few fronds of fern. Our consideration for the morals of the public is only equalled by our eagerness to go as far as we decently may in the other direction. What's your name?'

'Hazel Fairweather. I don't know yours either.'

'Paul Heritage. Is it tidier in the newspaper business than in ours?'

'I don't think so. We have to hunt down people who've been bereaved or attacked in lonely lanes, and make them talk about it. Sometimes they won't see us. Sometimes they cry. Sometimes they're just dying to tell us all about it. I think that's even worse.' She smiled wryly. 'But those are the plums of our profession. They don't happen every day.'

'What does happen every day, just people advertising for bicycles?'

'No,' said Hazel recklessly. 'That also was one of the plums.'

Paul turned to look at her face, but Hazel was gazing intently at the light coming through the tree-tops.

'The light can be dazzling at times,' said Paul.

'Yes,' admitted Hazel, who could have used a few fronds of fern just at the moment.

'The average day must be very humdrum indeed,' said Paul. 'How about the average Sunday?'

'On Sundays I help Daddy in the garden, unless it rains.'

'Oh, it won't rain.'

It didn't.

Paul arrived at the little house up at Pennyfold on his bicycle in time for midday dinner and endeared himself at once to Mrs. Fairweather by liking everything she had cooked and eating a lot. As he did not know a weed from a seedling it took him longer to win Mr. Fairweather's heart, but once having established that everything in a lawn that was not recognizably grass must be a weed, he fell happily to work. Hazel found him when he had painstakingly denuded the lawn of several inches of close-sown clover.

'Are you sure this is a weed,' he asked doubtfully. 'It's going to look pretty bald when I've got it all out.'

'It's clover. It comes in the lawn mixture.'

'Oh dear. How about daisies?'

'I should let them be. Just stick to dandelions and yarrow.'

'Yarrow?'

'This pretty feathery thing. You can't go wrong with that and Daddy loathes it.'

'Splendid. That'll keep me happy for hours.' He rolled over on to his stomach and began to weed yarrow in earnest. Mr. Fairweather unobtrusively fell asleep in a deck chair in the sun. Hazel passed with a wheelbarrow.

'Come and weed over here by me,' said Paul.

She flopped on the grass beside him and began to raise her own pile of yarrow. 'What do the others do on Sundays?' she asked.

'Lars has gone back to town to see a film at the Paragon in Leicester Square. One or two will have gone over to film shows in Bratton or Watchett. The rest will go to one of the three cinemas in Steeple Tottering. You'd think they'd want to look at real life for a change or even live it. Perhaps they daren't.'

'Why not?'

'For fear it should creep into their work. Or perhaps for fear they should see how wide the gulf is and not be able to bridge it.'

'But aren't they good?'

'Yes, they're all the best of their kind. They're turning out a good picture too. And I'm part of it. I shouldn't despise them, should I?'

'I don't see why not. I think some aspects of local journalism are pretty grim, but I get my living out of it. I expect everyone feels the same about their job to some extent.'

'They don't. Take Elizabeth. She honestly believes

64

the work she does is the result of inspiration—she who was born to be a provincial housewife, and has no qualifications whatsoever for anything but twins and a washing-machine and perhaps a television set.'

'Maybe you wouldn't call it a qualification, but she *is* beautiful.'

'Beauty is an accident,' said Paul. 'Anyhow, I don't like beautiful women.'

Hazel's heart leapt. And then he told her about the women he did like, about the woman he loved, and it wasn't Hazel.

'You can look at a beautiful woman like Elizabeth for ten minutes and know everything about her. You can guess exactly what cliché she'll use to greet every crisis that could confront her in her lifetime. The woman you want to know more about is the one that you never could really know anything about, however long you knew her. Her features could be unremarkable—even quite irregular—only you'd never be certain even of that because your eyes would dazzle whenever you looked at her or whenever you heard her voice. That's more than beauty.'

Hazel weeded for dear life. 'Had you anyone particular in mind?'

'I first came across it in 1938 when I was taken to see a play called "The Moment of Truth." Angela Wingless was in it. I can't tell you if the play was good or bad, but her every movement and every word were the very breath of magic; magic too strong for a boy of sixteen, I suppose.' Paul pursued a yarrow root brutally into the earth and withdrew it triumphantly. 'I saw her again next year in "So Fair—So Faithful." It was quite different, so different she almost broke my heart, but it didn't run; and I saw her twice in the next thing, "The Blossoming Thorn." '

'I saw that,' said Hazel. 'It was the first year of the war.'

'She was married to Bernard Taske then. He was younger than she, and wealthy. I suppose you'd call him a playboy. I didn't see her again till she came out to the front, when I was twenty-one. Did a show almost in the front line without props or footlights. We were all fagged out and most of the men would have rather had a leg show. She must have been exhausted too, and probably scared. But the magic still held. For nearly two hours she kept all thoughts of war and death at bay, and by the time the pieces of sacking that served for a curtain had swished together, there was hardly a man who wouldn't have said his prayers to her. I wrote to her that night.'

Paul moved a few feet and started weeding a fresh patch of lawn.

'I thought I was going to die within the next twenty-four hours and I had to write to somebody, but it wasn't the sort of letter to write home. She answered. I suppose I blackmailed her into it. I wasn't killed and I wrote again. She replied again, quite unguardedly, the sort of letter you'd write to a friend. We corresponded regularly after that, with extraordinary intimacy. I think the fact that she'd never seen me and probably never would, set her free to confide things she couldn't have told anyone else. She was afraid her husband had stopped

loving her and seemed desperately lonely. Then there
was a divorce. Taske had been having an affaire with a
friend of hers and I suppose this had made her distrust
everyone close to her. There was only me—for a time.
And then the letters got fewer, scrappy, detached.' He
smiled wryly, reminiscently. 'That must have been
when she first met Lars. I suppose that, whatever he
lacks, he gave her something of the companionship and
reassurance—something of the plain human warmth,
that she needed just then. What she gave him, that he
was able to appreciate, I can't imagine, a sort of
prestige, perhaps, comparable to marrying into the
aristocracy.' Paul's face grew bitter. 'Whatever it was
he does his best to destroy it whenever he mentions her
name.'

Weeding automatically Hazel asked, 'Did she write
and tell you she was going to be married?'

'No. It was the week I was demobbed. I came home,
determined to screw up my courage and find her and
find out why her letters had changed. I read about it
in the papers. It had been a quiet wedding. I wrote
and wished her happiness and got a detached little
note, thanking me and hoping I should be at her new
first night, and come round after.'

'Were you?'

'Yes. It was "Illyria Revisited." She was radiant and
very, very moving.'

'I know. I was there too, at the first night . . .' The
hope that even for a moment the thought should cross
his mind that they two had been under the same roof
at the same time was stillborn.

67

'I didn't go round after,' he went on. 'I could see she was happy and there was nothing really to be said. I've never seen her again. I got on with learning to be an architect. I had to make up the time I'd lost during the war. I got a chance to do some architectural detail for a film and eventually moved into art direction. It absorbed all my energy. Last year she wrote to me again, a friendly little letter, as though there had never been any gap. There it was—the same shining sincerity, the same reality. It gave me the idea that the illusion must be beginning to wear thin. Now that I've started this job under Lars, I realize just how thin. He cheapens her with every breath.'

'Does Lars know that you—know one another?'

'Oh, I don't think so. I don't suppose he's ever positively unkind to her, but it's as though a pantomime horse had married a racehorse and had to disparage what it couldn't appreciate or understand. I'm sorry I took this job now, in a way, but it was the best thing I'd a chance of doing and I wanted to work on this story.'

'Does she say anything against him, or about him at all, in her letters?'

'Heavens no. She never mentions him at all. I get the feeling that she's lonely and astray again, and needs someone to understand her. And after all, it's something that she's chosen me for that.'

And something, I suppose, that you should have chosen me, thought Hazel, though the brightness had gone from the sun which burned steadily down, and her fingernails were depressingly black—and still she burrowed doggedly after the yarrow roots as though her life depended on it.

'Dear knows why I've had to unburden myself of all this to you,' he said a little shamefacedly. 'But then you told me everyone did it. It's that face of yours and that permanent look of expectancy.'

Hazel was glad that he wasn't looking at her face just then and quite pleased when her father arrived and admired their prowess and began to take a hand himself. 'I'll resow the bare patches in the autumn,' he said. 'It ought to be quite a lawn by next spring.'

He went on to give Paul a comprehensive history of the plot, how it had been under vegetables during the war and immediate post-war periods, how he'd only attempted to remake it into a lawn during the last three years, and all the difficulty he'd had with poor seed and worn-out equipment. He had clearly been looking for a keen lawn man like Paul for a long time and was delighted to have discovered him.

Over tea Mrs. Fairweather was inclined to treat Paul as Hazel's beau and to tell him of quaint incidents out of her childhood and show off her paces a little, until, by the time he departed, Hazel felt that the entire family had united to bore him beyond endurance and to throw her at the head of a man already so moon-dazzled by Angela that he only saw any other woman as a possible confidante. At the last, her father pressed him warmly to regard the place as a second home during the rest of his stay—quite clearly with the intention of getting the lawn finished, and her mother repeated the invitation with the equally clear intent of getting her daughter nicely off with such a very agreeable young man.

When Hazel had seen him a little way down the hill she sat on the grass and cried, and there, toiling home with an easel, a canvas and a large box of paints, Professor Mandrake came upon her.

'Just the person I wanted to see,' said Mandrake, flopping beside her rather clumsily.

'Go away,' said Hazel.

'But I'm in trouble,' said Mandrake, 'and I need advice. I need the brutal detachment and the clear eye of youth.'

'My eye isn't clear,' said Hazel, though it was getting clearer, 'and I'm not in the least young.'

'Nevertheless you can't refuse your advice,' said the professor, settling himself more comfortably. 'Now here is my problem; late in life—I do not need to tell you how late—I came to the conclusion that I was getting in a rut. I needed to expand, to release my inhibitions, to adventure. I therefore bought this cumbrous box of oil paints, this palette and a dozen sizeable canvases. I booked a room at the "George," here, and every day I go out into the country, determined to divest my mind of all preconceived ideas and satisfy my soul by flinging the paint on the canvas in obedience to my own inner promptings, to express myself and return to rest unburdened and relaxed.'

'That sounds all right,' said Hazel.

'Now look here.' He laid his still-wet canvas face upwards on the grass at their feet. 'Tell me, quite brutally, what you see.'

'A cow,' said Hazel, 'standing on a hillside, a distant view of the twisting steeple, a largish dock-plant and some nettles.'

'That's what I feared,' said Mandrake depressedly. 'And you've no idea how hard I try.'

'Yes, I can see you've tried. But wasn't that what you meant to paint?'

'Of course not.'

'Do you mean the cow wasn't there? It can't have got in by itself.'

'Oh no, the cow was there, and the steeple and the dock and the nettles. But that wasn't *how* I meant to paint them.'

'Wasn't it?'

'Now listen. I am a man who possesses an early Picasso, a Chirico and a small but authentic Matisse. That is art as I understand and appreciate it. Nothing that *looks* like anything at all. No, I do not imagine myself to be a painter in their class but, if that is the work I admire, what is this dreadful thing in my released subconscious that forces me to paint smaller and smaller, in niggling, painful detail, each leaf, each blade of grass, each hair on the cow's tail? I choose larger and larger canvases, larger brushes, I even endeavour to splash paint on with a palette knife, yet in the frenzy of creation unconsciously I reject the palette knife, the larger brushes, unknown to myself I find I have completed the picture with the smallest brushes in the set, and even those I find hamperingly large.'

'I see what you mean, now,' said Hazel. 'It has all

got rather into the bottom left-hand corner of the canvas too, hasn't it?'

'It has. And can you imagine my chagrin—local children, coming upon me at work, recognize instantly the thing I am attempting to paint. It's humiliating. It could never have happened to Picasso.' He leaned forward morosely with his elbows on his knees and his chin on his hands. 'What am I going to do?'

Hazel considered the problem. 'Well,' she suggested tentatively after a moment, 'the question seems to be whether you honestly enjoy the actual painting, while you're doing it. I don't mean afterwards, when you see what you've done and realize it wasn't what you intended, but at the time?'

Mandrake also considered. 'Yes,' he said at last. 'While I'm actually lost in the painting, I believe I'm blissfully happy. Anyhow, the time goes in a flash and I'm always ravenously hungry when I've finished.'

'Then do you know what I'd do?' asked Hazel. 'I'd give away all those canvases and the big brushes and the oil paints, and I'd buy a quite small block of fine art paper, some pencils and a box of good water-colours. And I'd concentrate on turning out perfectly exquisite flower and leaf paintings, with every thorn and every vein showing, and maybe, when you felt reckless, a butterfly or something, clinging to the stalk with fragile feet and quivering antennæ. Only get them in the middle of the paper if you can. Then I should think you'd feel fine.'

'I believe I should,' said Mandrake, 'but . . .'

'After all, nobody need ever know.'

'You're absolutely right,' said Mandrake. 'And even if I wanted to, I wouldn't dare show any of my friends this sort of thing. Do you know, I've even got a modest reputation as a connoisseur of modern art.' He smiled and relaxed cheerfully on the grass. 'I shall do exactly as you say. You see how right I was to insist on having your advice?'

Hazel gave him a sidelong look. 'You just wanted to stop me crying.'

'Nonsense,' said Mandrake. 'I was at a moment of spiritual crisis and you have resolved it. Now I can go on my way and you can go on crying.'

'I shall do nothing of the sort.'

'Then perhaps you could bring yourself to tell me why a young woman of such penetrating judgment and considerable charm as yourself should sit sobbing in the cool of the evening at the end of such a perfect day.'

'You'd only need one guess,' said Hazel.

'As a scientist I may need more. My training and my life's experience have taught me that the only true ills from which human beings can suffer are illness or lack of food and adequate shelter. All other sorrows are illusory.'

'Like painting things the way they really look, for instance?'

'You have me there. Shall we assume you are in love?'

'Yes, I suppose we can safely assume that.'

'And the object of your devotion is indifferent or espoused to another.'

'He's not espoused but he's so wildly in love with her that he can't even see anyone else.'

'Does she return his love?'

'He's never even met her. She is an actress—a magnificent actress. He's only seen her on the stage portraying wonderful women of infinite courage and charm. And she writes him the most gloriously sincere letters. Nothing else. He's never spoken to her. You can't compete with someone who isn't even there to make mistakes and do anything human. She's just the ideal woman whose garment he is unfit to touch. The moon out of reach.'

'Why haven't they met? She writes to him, you say?'

'She's married. Unhappily, naturally, to a man who doesn't understand her or appreciate her in the least.'

'Has she, by any chance, a name?'

'Angela Wingless.'

Mandrake narrowed his eyes and looked at the darkening sky. 'Angela Wingless; yes, yes, I have met her. I have spoken to her, not intimately, but during a broadcast. I think she would remember my face—that, at least, is one of its advantages. She is, as you say, a magnificent artist. And her letters are gloriously sincere. Would it be committing yourself too far to tell me the young man's name?'

'Paul Heritage.'

'Heritage? Isn't he one of the film unit that's staying at the "George"?'

'Yes.'

'A very pleasant young man with a bicycle and corduroy trousers?'

74

'Yes.'

'What a ridiculous situation. You have given me your advice which I shall take. Here, for what it is worth, is mine. Get that young man and his moon-out-of-reach together as quickly as possible and for as long as possible, preferably on a slow boat to China. After that behave as a normally attractive young woman knows how to behave and let nature take its course. He'll be yours inside a week.'

'I don't think it's very good advice,' said Hazel. 'And even if it were, it's not very easy to put into practice. But thank you. I think I must go home now.'

'Perhaps I shall think of something else,' said Mandrake getting up and helping her to her feet. 'If I do, shall I tell you?'

'Yes, please.'

She turned and went back up the hill in the gathering dusk. At the last corner before she turned into her own lane, she almost bumped into a couple walking slowly with their arms round one another. One of them was Wormwell's curly-headed daughter. The other was Lars Porsen.

4

Mother may I go out to swim?
Yes, my darling daughter.
Hang your clothes on the hickory bush
But don't go near the water.

DURING the following week Hazel evolved her System of Absolute Honesty with Herself. In order to maintain her opinion of herself it was clear that she must not pursue Paul. Pursuing him consisted in taking the winding road past the location site at any time but when it was the quickest route between two necessary points. At all other times she must take the steep road past the Toad Rock and the Roman Barrow.

This she observed scrupulously, and since it entailed a swift descent past the Toad in the early mornings, when Paul was unlikely to be about, and the gentler climb, pushing the bicycle past Wimpley Water in the evening, when the chances were he would be just leaving the location, it was grossly unfair that she didn't run into him at all. On the other hand, there was a certain amount of tension in the office. Beasley, whose awaited heir continued not to arrive, though now ten

days overdue, was throwing all his pent-up energies
into trying to sell 'linage' stories in the hope of making
a little needed extra money.

During his newspaper career Beasley had established
connections with most of the London papers, so that by
asking for a reversed charge call to the news desk of any
of the papers, he could be sure of a hearing for any news
story and, if it were used, of a modest cheque. Since
no one else in the office attempted freelance work and
the calls cost the office nothing, Lightbody was agreeable for him to do it, so long as Beasley's calls were not
made during busy hours. Beasley, however, was needed
at home after office hours, and so, early in her employ-
ment, he had asked Hazel if, as a beginner, she would
like an old hand to teach her the ropes of making
London calls. Hazel, eager to learn everything, had
agreed and was now learning the hard way. Beasley
would leave her with the paragraphs and half a dozen
telephone numbers just before the office officially closed
and expect that she would 'phone each story to each of
the papers before she left. Hitherto he had never produced more than one or two stories, and those, items
that were really quite likely to be used, but now, with
his expectant fatherhood heavy upon him, he was finding 'sermons in stones' and news in everything, even the
unlikeliest sources. Hazel was beginning to understand
the market and knew fairly accurately where to offer
snob appeal news about the local peer, 'human notes'
about cute animals or children, and attacked girls. Any
instrument of assault that was not positively identifiable
as a hatpin naturally became a 'cosh,' and was

swallowed whole by all except the highest sections of the press.

But in his zeal to provide for the signalled little one, Beasley was producing stories that were frankly pointless. Maisie had refused flatly to telephone his last batch and even Hazel had suggested that, unless he sent something a bit more startling, he might wear out his welcome.

The film unit had naturally provided one or two snips, and Beasley had hung around the location hopefully, but at the beginning of the second week of their stay, filming had grown more businesslike and, as the main sheep scenes were concluded and the humans went before the cameras, all local sightseers had been excluded. On Thursday Beasley said to Lightbody, 'I think there's something fresh going on over at Wimpley Water. They ordered me out of the meadow when I happened to look in this morning.'

'Well, they're entitled to,' said Lightbody. 'They've rented the field for a month.'

'Yes, but last week the whole town was there. Must be a story.'

'All right. Get it.'

'There's a man called Dobell on the gate, questioning everyone that wants to go in. I thought Hazel, being a friend of the author, might get in. . . . I did hear they were testing a local girl for one of the scenes. . . .'

'Did you? Well, what's Hazel doing? You finish it for her and let her get over on her bicycle.'

Fate, already clearly on her side, now loaded the dice by throwing Orlando in her path. He was delighted to see her. No, he had not exactly visited the site since they had gone there together. No, it was impossible for him to come with her this afternoon as he was expected back in his office, though he would be very interested to know how they were progressing. Unfortunately, the location was so far from the town.

Hazel had an idea. 'Why don't you ask if you can see the rushes, sometimes?' she suggested. 'I believe they run through what they've taken on a little screen they've rigged up in a projection room in the hangar. That's no distance at all and you'd see what they'd actually done.'

'Yes, I'd like to see that very much. Do you suppose I should be welcome?'

'I'm on my way to Wimpley Water now. Would you like me to ask? I could find out when they were showing the rushes and let you know.'

'It would be very kind of you, very kind indeed.'

Hazel felt a little dishonest as she remounted her bicycle, but now she had a message to the director from the author, and even if it did not gain entry for her it was a step in the right direction.

It worked. Dobell, on guard at the gate, could not actually remember where he had heard Orlando Hallam's name before, but since Hazel assured him he was the author of the 'original,' and since she had a convincing manner, he let her pass. The grass near the gate was worn away with the last two weeks' traffic of people and equipment, but most of the unit was out of sight. Hazel made her way across the meadow to the first small clump of trees and then on to the larger group which screened the basin of Wimpley Water. As she threaded her way through the coppice she heard the familiar instructions and ejaculations, then the smart shock of wooden clappers and then silence. She froze in the middle of a stride but a twig broke under her foot with more noise than she would have thought possible. She realized that she was not very far behind the camera, which was shooting away from her towards the spot Paul had shown her on the previous occasion, where the sunlight shafted down through the tree-tops to the pool.

Lightfooted over the moss came Elizabeth Brentbridge, barefoot and wearing the simple peasant dress of Petronella, the shepherdess. She moved to an exact spot at the water's edge and dropped to her knees, looking into the pool. Almost at once she was followed by Coram McCoram, magnificent now in short breeches and ripped leather jerkin thonged with leather. He knelt behind her, immensely taller, till her eyes met his in the water and she turned, still kneeling.

'I told you not to come,' said Petronella.

'I won't look,' said the superb creature. 'I'll close my eyes. Only let me stay and listen to the water kissing your little feet—that I'm not worthy to touch.'

His eyes were shut. Petronella's face softened for a moment. 'You'll keep them shut—you promise?'

'Yes, if you'll tell me, with a kiss, when I may open them.'

Petronella touched his eyelid with one finger, then she moved quickly through the bushes and out of sight. Still with his eyes shut the splendid young man stretched backwards on the moss, where a second shaft of sun-light bathed his male magnificence in dazzling light. Hazel observed that some more of the larch tops had been sacrificed for this.

'Cut!' cried Lars Porsen.

The technicians went into a huddle. Coram McCoram sat up and the make-up man dashed in and patted his face with a velvet pad. He tugged at the neck of his jerkin. 'This leather is sawing my collar-bone,' he said.

Hazel sat down quickly exactly where she was stand-ing. If she didn't sit down now, they might start another take and she be frozen again into a position that was impossible to hold. Lars clearly wouldn't be ready to listen to any message for some time, and the main point was that she was here.

Mercedes had moved towards McCoram. 'I still think it ought to open lower,' she said. 'It only wants a couple of slashes with the scissors and a bit of Max Factor on the edges to darken them down.'

'That's what I said all along,' said McCoram grate-fully. 'Then a fellow could breathe. What do you say, Lars?'

'You do look a bit like a trussed fowl,' agreed Lars. 'Okay, Mercy, take the scissors to it.'

McCoram's torso was duly exposed to the air and McCoram breathed more freely.

Paul and Hollinshead moved back from the scene and almost trod on Hazel, obliterating her view. 'Well, he's achieved his plunging neckline again,' said Paul wickedly.

'I think he's right about it,' protested Hollinshead.

'Anyway, this is the best thing he's done since he started in pictures.'

'It's the best thing any of us has done,' said Paul. 'But is it good enough?'

'You always get that sort of feeling when a thing really begins to take shape,' said Hollinshead. 'A feeling that it's so good you're afraid you'll spoil it somehow. It's a sight healthier than feeling that you don't give a darn if you do.'

At this point he actually did tread on Hazel and turned to regard her with surprise.

'It's all right,' said Hazel. 'I came with a message for Mr. Porsen.'

'Well, for heaven's sake don't give it to him now.'

'Of course I won't. I'll wait till he's finished.'

'That's right,' said Hollinshead, sitting beside her.

'And don't get hiccups,' said Paul, sitting on her other side, 'in the middle of a take.'

The possibility of getting hiccups in the middle of a take had never occurred to Hazel, but now it had been suggested it seemed inevitable. Paul gave her a dazzling smile that put all minor considerations out of mind. 'You see how nicely I did the sunshine?' he said.

'All by yourself?' The words bubbled out before she could stop them. 'I hope you rested on the seventh day.'

'No, actually, I put in the hardest afternoon of my life on the seventh day, pulling yarrow out of a lawn, and the saddening thing is I can't stop now. Whenever I sit on a patch of grass I automatically weed it clear of yarrow without knowing I'm doing it. The sheep think

82

I'm just another sheep—only, of course, in wolf's clothing. They nudge me and tell me all sorts of things.'

His hand fell on hers with sudden urgency, and her heart had leapt in a frenzy of rapture before she realized that the scene was being taken again and that she had been deaf this time to the warning cries and the clapper-boy and everything but the sound of Paul's voice. When it was done she said, 'Who is the young man?'

'Coram McCoram,' said Hollinshead. 'I thought every girl in Great Britain knew that torso.'

'Yes, of course I knew. I mean what is he playing?'

'Peter the Poacher, of course,' said Hollinshead.

'But—I'd supposed Peter the Poacher was someone quite rough and unattractive, who only came into the story when she went to bathe in the big reservoir down near the town.'

'Did you?' asked Hollinshead. 'Well you have to have twists and new angles in a film script. This way they're childhood sweethearts. Makes it all much more poignant later on.'

'Yes, I see. Does she go into the water now?'

'I think so,' said Hollinshead. 'Lars isn't retaking on that. Yes, she goes into the pool for a moment and then you see her on the bank, getting into her dress and running off through the trees. There's a sort of freshness about it that's something rare in pictures . . . ssh . . .'

For they were taking again. The camera was trained on the centre of the pool, where in the deepest water, the laughing, virginal creature was revealed for a moment, naked, in the leaf-filtered sunlight, behind a carefully-placed arrangement of bracken fronds. She took two strokes in the rippling, crystal water, then, 'Cut!' cried the director.

'And when Peter opens his eyes at last she isn't there,' explained Hollinshead. 'There's just a sheep that has followed her into the water and he's been listening to it splashing, not her at all.'

Elizabeth was being shrouded into enormous towels on the bank and stood, waiting to know if there would be a retake.

'Mario Fideli's music for this is really inspired,' whispered Hollinshead.

Even the technicians had begun to speak in muted voices, for the lovely scene, with no word spoken, no gesture or expression in poor taste, coupled with the girl's unaffected beauty and the music of the dimpled water had hushed them into reverence and even brought tears into some of their Kleig-weary eyes. They felt that the cumbersome film machinery and the incongruous ingredients had combined to entrap on celluloid a moment of genuine innocence and Hazel caught a little of the elation that she saw on all their faces.

Paul had gone over to the pool-side and was readjusting one of the bracken fronds. 'I expect they'll retake,' said Hollinshead, 'though it looked perfect to me. You see, quite apart from its intrinsic charm this sequence explains why Peter the Poacher, later when he's come to full manhood, is angry and jealous when he learns that she, who regarded herself as too pure for his touch, is now willing to bathe naked in the public reservoir, and why he feels compelled to take the glimpse of her that was denied him then. Naturally it makes the final sequence when she dedicates her life and the use of her eyes to him, doubly poignant too. The whole thing hangs together beautifully in the script.' He smiled wryly and his voice changed. 'Not that anyone will get much credit for it except Lars,' he muttered on an even lower note.

Hazel remembered why she had come. 'Do you suppose Mr. Hallam would be able to see any of the material they've taken? Don't they sometimes run off the previous day's shots in the hangar?'

'Yes, as a matter of fact Lars has planned to run through everything we've taken so far in the projection room to-morrow. They don't really like outsiders, but they can hardly call Hallam that.'

'Would it be safe for me to ask?'

'I should think so. Lars couldn't be in a better mood. Wait till he's finished taking for the day, though.'

Some sort of lull had come to pass. Mercedes came and spoke to Hollinshead, then she regarded Hazel with surprise. Hazel thought it might be a good idea to pay her the seven and sixpence for the Caribbean Orchid lipstick, and Mercedes, softened, sat on the grass and told her it became her well.

'How did that last take look from here?' asked Mercedes. 'Frightful, isn't it? Those collar-bones.'

'I don't know,' protested Hazel. 'You can't really see his collar-bones from here.'

'His?' Mercedes looked closely at Hazel. 'His are all right. I meant her.'

'Well, they're fixing some more bracken,' said Hazel, deciding to play for safety, 'so it ought to be all right.'

'It'll have to be all right before Lars passes it,' said Mercedes. 'And I will say he knows how to handle this sort of thing, even with her. Doesn't let her speak a word in the shot.'

'There isn't any dialogue in the script just there,' said Hollinshead with a flicker of spirit.

'And whose script is it?' said Mercedes.

'Even Lars can't say I didn't do most of the dialogue.'

'And because you *didn't* write the dialogue that she *doesn't* speak you feel you ought to take credit for the scene.'

Hazel felt the conversation could continue on these lines indefinitely, but she hesitated to move nearer the camera and it seemed a pity to move further away. She began to wonder how long Lightbody would consider a legitimate time for her to spend in search of a local story and recalled that she had not, in any case, discovered one. When Mercedes had delivered a more or less final blow in the apparently quite usual conversation Hazel turned to her again.

'I suppose Mr. Porsen hasn't come across anyone local who's likely to be used in the picture, has he?'

'No.' Mercedes was instantly alert. 'Has anyone said he has?'

'Only some gossip I heard, that one of the children might be going to be used.'

'Who said so? Peggy Wormwell?'

'Only gossip,' Hazel repeated. 'She was here with her father the other day, wasn't she? She seemed a lively little thing.'

'She's lively enough to make a fool of herself, telling people she's going to be in the picture.'

'Isn't she, then?'

'Of course not. Lars may be a perfect fool over *children*, letting her stand in range and go through a few grimaces while he worked the camera, but he's not a fool over *pictures*. There wasn't any film in it.'

'Did she think there was?'

'Not unless she's quite crazy. And if she is she's only herself to blame.'

So there was no local story at all. Hazel asked about the sheep and learned that they had completed their scenes the previous day and would not be required again until after the unit had moved down to the Sallow Water reservoir for the big moment of the picture when Petronella's body was changed into dazzling light as it plunged into the water.

They were taking again and Mercedes dashed back to her post; presently Paul returned and, stooping a little, with one hand on the silver birch tree beside Hazel, he said:

> 'Come away, oh human child
> To the waters and the wild,
> From a world more full of weeping than
>   you can understand.'

Hazel came. He guided her through the coppice until they were out of earshot of the cameras and then began to talk as he walked. 'I was coming to see you yesterday evening.'

'Oh.'

'Only when I got back to the "George" there was a letter for me that had come by the afternoon post, from Angela.'

'So you stayed at the "George" and spent the evening answering it.' It was not a question.

'Yes. She's unhappy again; quite openly now. I'd never supposed Lars was physically unfaithful to her, but I'm not even sure of that. It's destroying for a woman of her quality.'

'How do you know?'

'I don't know. Do you remember I told you Lars was going up to town at the week-end? Well, he can't have gone. Or at least he can't have gone home to Angela. She said she'd expected him and what a lonely time she'd had, and asked me why we let him work so hard at the picture.'

'Did you tell her in your letter that he wasn't working on the picture?'

'No. Should I have? I couldn't make up my mind. I wrote one letter telling her exactly what I thought of his treatment of her, but I tore that up quite early. In the end I just wrote a completely non-committal one about the place and the work and telling her I'd met you.'

'That must have been *just* what she hoped for.'

'Do you think she'd be jealous?'

'Not if you described me accurately. In twenty-two years I've never stirred up an atom of jealousy in any female bosom except when I won the Head's prize for Composition in my last year.'

'I believe you're right,' said Paul in a voice of pleased

discovery. 'Even Mercedes who's as spiteful as a harpy about every other woman seems perfectly friendly to you.'

'Don't you realize why?' said Hazel with a three-cornered smile. 'I don't offer any competition. I might just as well not be there.'

Paul stopped in his long stride and stood looking down at her thoughtfully. 'No. It isn't that at all. It's something altogether different and nobody has it but you.'

Hazel felt happiness lifting her heart and the corners of her mouth and beginning to glow on her face, and for fear he also should notice so much on such slight provocation she spoke quickly.

'Why didn't you give Lars away to Angela?'

'I didn't know what to do. I don't want to make her unhappy unless she has to be. What would you have done?'

'It depends how much I minded. If I minded as much as I think you do I should play every card I'd got and make a bid for her myself.'

'Would you? No, I don't think *you* would. And, if I did, what cards have I got that would help?'

'Lars didn't go to London at the week-end. I saw him up on Pennyfold just as dusk was falling. He had his arm round one of the village girls.'

'What? Oh, surely not? Heavens, if he had to run amok, let him at least do it among his own class and kind with people who understand the rules.' His face was bitter. 'And, if I were to play a card like that, what do you suppose Angela would do?'

'Divorce him and marry someone of her own class

and kind—if she were asked—someone who'd appreciate her and make her happy.'

'It might be,' said Paul, gazing away towards the horizon, 'it might be indeed, but how could I humiliate her by ever letting her know he could come so low as that. If she lost him to another actress, even Elizabeth, say, or someone her own stature, yes, she could possibly endure it and keep her head up—but a roll in the long grass with the farmer's daughter, no. Could you hurt someone you—cared about, like that, even if it gave you a chance of getting them for yourself? I'd rather just preserve any fool's paradise that's left to her by saying nothing—until . . .'

'Until she finds out for herself?'

'Or something like that.'

A bellow broke across the meadow and they realized that shooting had finished. 'I want to ask Lars Porsen if Orlando can see the rushes to-morrow,' said Hazel.

'Come along and tackle him now, then. He's as mellow as a peach this afternoon.'

Lars was already half-way across the meadow full of goodwill to mankind, and promised cheerfully, even extending the invitation to Hazel so long as she swore on her heart to use nothing she saw in her paper. Hazel, aware that her paper's interest only went as far as Wormwell's sheep, promised willingly. Then Lars announced he was off for his daily communion with nature, vaulted the gate and got into his car.

'See you in the rushes,' he called out wittily, 'as Pharaoh's daughter said to Moses,' and drove up the hill.

Hazel bicycled as slowly as possible downhill, hoping that Paul's bicycle might overtake her, but Paul had got caught up in some discussion with Bertrand and she saw no more of him. She stopped at the Catchment Board Office to tell Orlando that he would be welcome at the projection room in the hangar at half-past four on Friday, and then went to her own office to report a complete blank on local girls making good. She decided not to make any mention of 'Elizabeth Brentbridge—Bare' to Beasley, since though unquestionably the best of material for one of his London paragraphs, she felt that to mention it would be a breach of privilege. Friday afternoon was always slack in the office and she knew that by working through the lunch hour she stood a chance of getting off in time to see the 'rushes.'

Half-past four next day duly found her in the projection room with most of the unit. Lars was in front and Hazel heard Hollinshead, who was beside him, saying, 'I believe Anglia-Rokewood are after him for their next picture. They start about the twenty-seventh.' Lars looked concerned but Hazel couldn't hear any more. Mercedes squeezed in beside her and pointed out that Orlando, in what he had doubtless regarded as the safe obscurity of the back row, was going to interfere sadly with projection. As soon as the machine began to whirr, someone called out to him to put his head down and there he huddled, screwed between chairs in uncomplaining discomfort, throughout the showing. When the clapper-boy with his striped and numbered board appeared, Mercedes whispered,

'That all comes out in the cutting. You're seeing something nobody ever sees.'

The first shots of weary sheep and shepherds toiling up rocky winding paths seemed interminable and interminably repeated. At last it came to the scene she had seen photographed that day with Orlando, where the little flocks drank at the hallowed spring and were restored to health.

A stertorous breath behind Hazel's ear, which had seemed to be muttering dissatisfaction, now changed and murmured, 'Pretty as a picture, they be,' and was shushed by Mercedes. Hazel turned and deciphered the rugged outline of farmer Wormwell in the gloom. The film purred on, then stopped, then started again. A group of character actors dressed as shepherds played a short scene, then knelt by their stricken flocks. A bell-ringer passed through the town's cobbled market-place, which had been photographed empty on early closing day, crying that the flocks must be burnt. Now McCoram's physique began to intrude on the eye, and short scene followed short scene showing the dawning of his love and his innocent pursuit of the shepherdess. Last came the sequences that Hazel had watched on the previous day, where the camera lingered, almost with tenderness, on the idyllic beauty of the setting and the performers. The camera work was breathtakingly lovely. No icing rose on a wedding cake could have looked more flawless than the shepherdess, no man carved out of polished wood more splendidly virile than her lover.

As the film ended there was a hush of genuine feeling.

A light came on and revealed to Hazel the huddle of dusty chairs. Then in the silence, a low amazed voice from behind Hazel said, 'Be that all? Where be the rest of it?'

'Of course that's all,' snapped Mercedes sharply over her shoulder. 'And quite enough after only ten days' shooting in difficult locations like these.'

'But where be the pictures he took of Peggy? Do 'e mean to tell oi there baint no pictures of Peggy?'

'Of course there aren't,' said Mercedes with finality. 'You be grateful your sheep are all there where they ought to be.'

'But 'e praamised my daughter . . . and for that my daughter praamised oi . . .' then the words came in a crumbling roar, 'There 'e be at the end of the row . . . and 'e'll answer to me for me daughter . . .'

As Wormwell's voice rose to a roar and he started to stumble past the other people in his row, Hollinshead and Gussie closed round Lars and began to hustle him out of the projection room.

Hazel started to follow them and was knocked flying by the farmer in his endeavour to get through the door first. Her head caught the wooden seat of a chair and she sprawled on the floor, stunned. Mercedes and one or two others tripped over her in the gloom but still hurried on. Paul, stepping over the chair backs from the last row but one, picked her up and helped her out into the yard. Lars had vanished and Wormwell was swaggering about looking baffled.

'Put your arm round my shoulder and I'll get you into the car,' Paul said, hoisting her into his arms, and in a moment she was in the two-seater. He started it up and stopped when they were out of the town. He regarded her with solicitude. 'Sorry I had to bump you about,' he said, 'but if I hadn't got the car out of range someone else would have claimed it. Just relax a bit and then I'll drive you home.'

Hazel smiled dazedly. 'I'm all right,' she said. 'Thanks. I'm really all right now.'

5

*A little amateur painting in water-colour shows
the innocent and quiet mind.*

                                    R. L. STEVENSON

*Sweet chance, that led my steps abroad,
    Beyond the town, where wild flowers grow.*

                                    W. H. DAVIES

P AUL considered the situation for a moment, then,
'Shall I drive on a bit?' he asked.

'Yes, please.'

He drove on up till they were level with the Toad
Rock. Then he stopped the car at the side of the road
and got out. He opened the door on Hazel's side and
together they crossed the grass between the Roman
Barrow and the rock and stood at the brink of the drop,
looking down across the town.

'I've been wanting to do this ever since I've been
here. There's a magnificent view.'

'Yes. This mound is supposed to be a Roman barrow,
only no one's thought to dig it up and see yet. And that
rock is called the Toad. It's the local "dare".'

The stone was large, flattish on the top and curved
below in an ellipse so that only a small surface of the
stone came in contact with its equally smooth bed of

rock. Close velvet turf covered the ground except for the bare patch immediately below the Toad, which was poised, it seemed, most precariously at the very brink of a low ravine. The barrow, to its left, made a sun-warmed hollow between itself and the rock, sheltered from the wind, screened from the road, carpeted with short turf and ideally situated for lovers.

'Dares,' said Paul cheerfully regarding the rock, 'are the point at which my moral courage breaks even with my physical cowardice. I have enjoyed a long and comparatively useful life on the principle of always refusing to do anything I am dared.'

'How sensible,' said Hazel.

'In fact,' Paul continued, 'if it depended on me, no silk hats would appear on Eros' statue, the summit of Brazenose College would remain for ever unpotted and birds could do their damnedst to Nelson from this time forth. I have a yellow streak. I like it that way.'

'But you climbed to the top of that tree to cut down some branches at Wimpley Water.'

'Not for fun. Besides, I didn't look down or think about anything but the fact that I had to get the light right. That was business. Pleasure is something else again and should only consist of things you really enjoy.'

'It's odd when you think how simple life can be for anyone who has the courage to develop their own character and keep it like that. You've made me realize that everyone who lets themselves be stampeded into doing something useless and dangerous, for a dare, is just a show-off. I wish I had some of your moral courage.'

'Ah, but you need my physical cowardice as well. One is useless without the other.'

'I've got that all right. I was nearly sick when they dared me to rock the Toad.'

His lashes shadowed his eyes for a moment. 'And you did it?'

'I'm afraid so.' She saw her mistake too late.

'Oh, damn you.'

'I'd have more sense now. Even the local girls have given up daring their boys. They'd rather have a seat at the pictures.'

He wasn't listening. 'What did you have to do?'

She didn't answer.

He took her hand and led her to the Rock. 'Tell me,' he said.

'Those two slight depressions on the top are the foot-holds. You put your left foot here in the near one and your right foot in the far one so that you straddle the centre. Then very gradually you transfer your weight to the right foot and the rock sways with you till it feels as though it will tip you right off into space, and at that exact moment you lean your weight back again on to your left foot and the rock sways back to where it is now. Daredevils spread their arms wide and rock it a couple of times, but once is enough for most people. It was for me.'

'Like this?' asked Paul, scrambling up and putting his left foot in the first worn place. There was no dare-devilry on his face, only a fixed determination.

'Don't,' said Hazel, but Paul's right foot had moved to the second hold and he was spreading his arms and transferring his weight gradually to the right foot. The rock swayed sickeningly and the ravine swung below him. '*Now!*' cried Hazel. 'Come back now.' Paul brought his weight back on to the left foot, waited till his balance was steady and then rocked the whole thing forward again, stepping back at the last second. He jumped quietly on to the base rock and took one step. Then his legs crumpled under him and he sprawled on the turf on the right of the rock.

Hazel sat beside him.

'I'm not sitting here on purpose,' he said. 'My legs have given way.'

'I know. Why did you do it?'

Paul began to grin shamefacedly. 'In the light—of my previous statements,' he said, still having difficulty with his breathing, 'there doesn't seem to be any answer. I suppose man is a more primitive animal than I had imagined.'

Hazel thought, 'Does he mean he did it because he couldn't let me down by being a coward, or just that he had to show his male supremacy over any woman?' But she said, with her eyes glowing, 'Woman is not without her primitive side also.'

'Let's face it,' he said briskly, 'it feels exactly as though the whole rock is going to roll over the top into the next world. Doesn't it ever?'

'It hasn't, so far.'

'Suppose you had a stiff leg or got cramp and couldn't step back?'

'I'd rather not suppose it.'

'Suppose someone rolled a smaller rock under it at the near side, so that it wouldn't rock back?'

'You'd lose your balance and go over.'

'Hasn't there ever been an accident?'

'Yes. A man was killed in nineteen thirty-nine. I believe there was a movement in the town at the time to have the rock dynamited off into the valley once and for all, but the war took everyone's mind off and nobody's thought about it since.'

Silence fell between them and a bee bumbled into the rock and away again. As they lay, half in the rock's shadow, half in sunlight, Hazel was trying to print the moment in her mind and keep it for ever. 'Soon he will go away and get on with his life and I must get on with mine. This is all I shall ever have, this moment and perhaps one or two more before the unit leaves. And if he suspected how much it meant to me there mightn't be any more moments. I'm sure he's the honourable type who wouldn't willingly trifle with anyone's affections. If only I could ever look at his face long enough to be sure I'd always remember it, without him catching me at it and realizing how I felt.'

She lifted herself on her elbow and turned to look at him, and then she smiled. With a totally preoccupied face, he was busily weeding yarrow out of the turf. The pulled weeds lay in a neat little pile and were already wilting in the sunshine. She watched his lean, sensitive fingers and his fine-boned, intelligent head until suddenly he turned, met her eyes and looked back at his pile of weeds. Then he laughed.

'If seven maids with seven mops swept it for half a
    year,
Do you suppose, the Walrus said, that we should get
    it clear?'
said Hazel.

'I didn't realize I was doing it. I was thinking about
life.'

'Oh. Then you probably *will* get it clear before you
reach a conclusion.'

Hazel recalled that she had not looked at her face
since Paul had picked her off the dusty floor of the
projection room. She opened her bag and cleaned off a
little dust with her handkerchief and put on some fresh
lipstick. She screwed the top on to the ornate Caribbean
Orchid case and, as she reached for her powder case,
the lipstick slipped out of her hand and rolled under
the Toad. She groped under the rock with her fingers,
but it had rolled in to where the aperture became too
narrow for her to reach it.

'What's wrong?' said Paul.

'My lipstick. It's rolled right under. I could get it
with a stick or something.'

'Is it the one Mercedes wished on you? Because if so,
now it can be told.'

'What can?'

'It doesn't suit you a bit. Mercedes has been trying
to palm that bad buy off on somebody ever since she
bought it herself. I should let it lie.'

'Oh dear,' said Hazel. 'Do I look funny or just
vulgar?'

He put a warm, if earthy, hand over hers. 'Neither,

you cherub. Just not quite so gentle as you looked in the train the first day I saw you.'

'Oh, that was the "Maidenbloom." I haven't used it up yet. Do you think I'd do better to revert?'

'If my personal preference has anything to do with it, yes. Shall I take you home now?'

Paul's personal preference had everything to do with it. As he got to his feet a car came over the top of the hill and stopped below the barrow. Paul sat down again. 'It's Lars,' he said, 'on his way to commune with Nature. Don't let's bump into him and spoil the day.'

Lars came into view over the top of the mound, then he moved down into the hollow on the far side of the Toad from them, stretched a moment, yawned in the sun, took out a florid silk handkerchief, spread it on the turf and lay down with it under his cheek. In a moment he was asleep.

'I might have known it,' whispered Paul, stepping silently over the grass to his own car. 'If he were going to commune with nature or anything else, he wouldn't insist on being alone. He'd want an audience. He just comes here to take a nap.'

Hazel got into the car. 'Why doesn't he take a nap in his room?'

'I don't know. Yes, I do. It's just over the four-ale bar where the darts teams play. The noise is terrific.'

'But someone offered to change rooms with him that day I had lunch in the "George" and he refused.'

'I suppose it was a matter of pride. He goes around

being younger and fitter than the youngest of us. It might call his bluff a bit to own up to needing a nap.'

'What does he do when it rains?'

'It's only rained once since we've been here. And come to think of it, that evening he was as irritable as could be over his dinner. Poor man, he'd be furious if he thought we knew.'

Paul let in the clutch, smiling, and drove Hazel up to Pennyfold and stopped at her door. Then he waved to her, backed the car on to the grass and drove off down the hill. When he had gone Hazel remembered that she had meant to find out if he would be going to London for the week-end or if he too would be at the party at the 'George' to which Elizabeth Brentbridge had invited Hazel and Mr. Hallam that day on location. She never remembered the things she meant to say to Paul until it was too late.

On the following morning she stopped at the tobacconist's to buy a quarter of her month's chocolate ration, twenty cigarettes, and two packets of book matches. She did this every Saturday and, if she ran out before the following Saturday, did without. As nobody in her office was honourable about matches she always wrote her name on the flap of the book. It didn't prevent people pocketing them, but she hoped it might at least trouble their conscience.

When she got to the office she found Beasley running a temperature. The stork had been positively hovering over his house since the small hours of the morning and any minute now he would be a father. Hazel gave him several of her cigarettes and a small bit of her chocolate at intervals during the morning. It seemed the least she could do and he appeared to feel the same. Lightbody told him the joke about the maternity doctor who said he'd never lost a father yet, but it wasn't well received. Beasley went home at lunch-time and came back disconsolate and very hungry. Zero hour was still to come. Nobody had seemed to notice that the master was home and the matter of his dinner had not been broached. Lightbody gave him three and six out of the petty cash and sent him to have lunch at the 'George.'

When Beasley had not returned by half-past four, Lightbody began to regret his generous impulse and cast his eye over the office's wall calendar, on which appointments that could be predicted in advance were scribbled from day to day. 'Holy smoke!' he cried suddenly. 'Horace Rivermead was marrying Grace Lessops this morning. Has anyone covered it?'

Nobody had. Grace Lessops was the daughter of Greg Lessops, Steeple Tottering's bank manager. Horace Rivermead's father owned a considerable saw-mill. History was being made and the *Sallowshire Guardian* had fallen down on it.

'Mr. Beasley was going to have covered it,' said Maisie. 'I suppose he forgot.'

'Well, I presume we sent the bride a form to fill in. Look it up, it should have all the details.'

'I took the form round on Wednesday but there wasn't anyone at home, so I put it through the letter-box.'

'Did you call round next day to collect it?'

'No, I suppose I can't have.'

'The reception was going to be at the "George",' said Hazel. 'Do you suppose Mr. Beasley will have remembered to get the details from one of the guests. Some of them are bound to be still there.'

'I don't suppose Beasley remembers his own name,' said Lightbody. 'Cut along to the "George," Hazel, tell Beasley to come back to his job while he's still got one and get any particulars you can about the wedding, there's a good girl.'

Hazel ran Beasley to earth in the lounge and gave him the message, slightly modified. She inquired for the wedding party and learned that it had retired, at closing hours, to the Chintz Parlour at the back. This was the room that had been more or less set aside for the use of the film unit, but, as the room was filled with members of both the wedding party and the film unit, it was clear that a compromise had been effected. In fact, Lars seemed to be running the proceedings, which were right down his street, and as Hazel entered he was in full flight, making a speech that left practically nothing unsaid that any bride or bridegroom would wish unsaid.

He dwelt lovingly and with rich double entendre on the matter of 'giving the bride away,' went into detail about the desirability of having a bank manager for a father-in-law, and then pointed out the convenience in a domestic crisis of having, on the premises, the requisite equipment for sawing a lady in half.

The bank manager then plunged into an interminable speech, and Lars lost interest in the whole matter.

'You've changed your lipstick back,' said Mercedes, who gave up listening the moment Lars stopped speaking.

Hazel felt guilty for no good reason at all. 'Yes, I lost the other one.'

'Where?'

'It rolled under the Toad too far for me to reach it yesterday evening.'

Lars had come over towards them as Mercedes was asking, 'What toad?' And now Paul, too, had joined the group.

'The Toad Rock,' Hazel explained. 'Haven't you come across it?'

'I don't know.'

'You must have seen it a dozen times,' said Paul. 'It commands the entire landscape . . . That rock, poised on the brink of the abyss, over towards Pennyfold.'

'Oh, I know,' said Lars. 'It's beside a sort of mound thing up on the hill.'

'That's it,' agreed Paul, with a glint of mischief in his eye. 'It's the local "dare." The spot where the maidens test their young men. The swains have to climb up and rock it to prove their manhood.'

'I know a better way,' said Lars.

'Of course you do,' said Paul. 'That's just for the foolhardy yokels, drunk with youth.'

There was a moment's pause, then:

'What do they have to do?' asked Lars.

'Hazel will show you. She did it herself once.'

Hazel demonstrated how one rocked the Toad and stepped back in the nick of time, then watched him glance at his watch, and heard him say, 'Well, so long to everyone and best of luck to the bride.' She saw him cross the floor and heard his car starting up and began feverishly taking down notes about the wedding.

Paul took out his pipe, packed it, got no flame from his lighter and looked round for a match. Even in the middle of her notes this fact communicated itself to Hazel and she handed him her book-matches without looking up.

'That is the worst of these cheap lighters,' said Mercedes, intending a joke, and started a desultory conversation. In a few moments the porter came in with a telegram for Paul. 'It's a reply-paid,' he said, 'the boy's waiting.'

Paul read it, looked pleased, then rather irritated, glanced at the clock and muttered, 'Handed in on Friday at five-forty-five . . . hasn't taken a minute more than twenty-four hours.' He got up and left the Chintz Parlour without another word.

Hazel got the rest of her facts, went back to her now deserted office and wrote up the wedding. Then she redid her face, pinned a white piqué flower on her office frock, read her horoscope in Maisie's magazine, and returned to the 'George' for Elizabeth Brent-bridge's party. Elizabeth had said 'any time after six-thirty,' so a quarter to seven had seemed about right to Hazel, but there was no one in the lounge and no one in the Chintz Parlour, which had not yet been tidied after the wedding reception and certainly did not suggest expected guests. Hazel had not assumed it to be a dinner party, but she opened the door of the dining-room a little timidly and looked inside. A few of the lesser members of the unit were dining, but not Elizabeth, not Lars, and not Paul. Hazel resigned herself to the fact that Elizabeth had forgotten all about her party ten minutes after she had issued the invitations, and was on her way out when she encountered Orlando just coming in, with his hair even flatter than usual and the nervous air of good manners which is apt to betray those on their way to parties and unaccustomed to them.

'Oh, Hazel,' said Mr. Hallam. 'I hope I'm not late.'

'I don't think so,' said Hazel. 'There's no one else about yet. Film people are notoriously unpunctual.' Hazel had an idea that film people couldn't afford to be unpunctual when wasted minutes could run them into hundreds of pounds, but she was doing her best at short notice. She would have preferred to creep away and never remind anyone she had been asked to a party, but something had to be done about Mr. Hallam.

'Why don't you sit in the lounge and I'll find out where they are?'

She deposited him in the lounge and went through the 'George' more thoroughly. This time she found Paul coming into the foyer. She told him what had happened. Paul took her arm.

'Come on,' he said, 'let's find Elizabeth. At least I'm sure she hasn't gone up to town. Her flat's being redecorated.'

He led her back into the dining-room and approached the unit table.

'Someone go and scare up Elizabeth while the rest of

you go into the lounge and start a party for Orlando Hallam. Elizabeth invited them ten days ago and she hasn't shown up. I'll go and wash my hands and then I'll join you.'

Hazel noticed that his hands were remarkably dirty, Gussie stood up and said, 'I'll go up and bang on her door. She's a dear girl, but vague. I expect she's forgotten all about it.' Hollinshead and Mercedes followed Hazel into the lounge and in a few moments Gussie came back with the message that Elizabeth had been fast asleep, but of course she'd be down at once and the party was to proceed. A waiter, under hurried instructions, shepherded them into the Chintz Parlour and started whipping off soiled linen and snack plates, overflowing ash-trays and glasses with dregs in them. If anything had been needed to remove the final gloss from the party, here they had it.

The conversation jolted wearily over how wonderful it must be to be an author and how did Orlando think up his ideas. Paul reappeared and did everything but stand on his head. He even remembered that Gussie knew a funny story and asked him to tell it. While he got his second wind he whispered to Hazel, 'You know this is one of the very few occasions when I would positively welcome Lars.'

At last Elizabeth wandered down and began to play hostess between stifled yawns. She asked where Lars had got to and when nobody knew she remarked that it was later than he usually returned. Then she noticed her photograph on an old number of a fan magazine on the escritoire and began to read what it had said about her. Forsaken by their last hope, even the well-intentioned were stricken to silence which was broken at last by an hysterical voice remarking that you could almost hear a pin-up girl drop.

Mandrake leaned forward on his precarious folding stool and lovingly traced the scroll of a woodbine tendril clinging to the stalk of a feathery head of hemlock. In the foreground there were three harebells, some 'Devil's bit Scabious' and a dock leaf, and in the background the bank of rock which supported the Toad. Of course, the Toad was too high up to come into his picture, but that was as well. Mandrake had learned that in his sort of painting there really was no necessity for distance or background, the foreground was so gloriously packed. He was almost perfectly happy. Of course he was aware that his pretence of having to go out into the countryside every day was the purest sophistry. He could have managed his subjects just as well if he had stuck a bunch of grasses and a few leaves and flowers into a tooth-glass and painted them in his bedroom, but the fun wouldn't have been the same and Mandrake was a painter for fun. Ah yes, a painter, he reminded himself, for to-morrow he would return, set up his easel again, open his water-colour box and hand-paint these delicious outlines with delicate colour. 'Hand-paint,' now, that was an odd term to come into his mind. The sort of term which would only suggest itself to a dealer in 'art' calendars and Christmas cards. Odd how one's subconscious could trip one up. He leaned back to appreciate his handiwork, then glanced at the background and away and then suddenly back. Surely there was an object on the ground which had not been there before. Something quite large and green and brown that huddled on the grass near the rocky bank, something quite still.

Lars lay twisted on the grass with one arm bent under him and one flung out, with his eyes horribly open, wearing his light-brown trousers and green sports jacket.

Mandrake loosened his tie and made certain he was dead, then after a brief investigation went back for his sketching equipment. He hurried down to the nearest place where he could climb up to the grass and came back up the road. He looked at the Toad for quite a time, and then back over the brink to the body below. Then he picked up a packet of book matches from the left of the Toad and sat down on the turf. He studied the grass very carefully and picked up two spent matches, torn from the book, but no cigarette ends. He found a little bare patch in the turf and a tiny pile of freshly-pulled weeds.

He got up and picked up his things and went off fairly briskly down the hill towards the town. At the edge of the town there was a telephone box. He went inside and told the police that there was a dead man lying at the foot of the ravine below the toad-shaped rock, and he was on his way in to make a statement if required, but he supposed they might wish to send an ambulance. Then he stopped at the 'George,' asked if any of the unit were there, and was directed to the Chintz Parlour, where he told the assembled company that their director lay dead at the foot of the Toad Rock.

Mercedes went into hysterics and insisted that they go up at once and find Lars, but Mandrake assured her it would be purposeless as a police car and an ambulance with a surgeon were already on their way up. Mercedes turned on Paul then, saying it was all his fault for talking so much about the Toad. A man of Lars' spirit could naturally not resist a challenge of that sort. Mandrake asked what she meant, and Mercedes explained that Paul had practically dared him to ride it.

'When?' asked Mandrake.

'Just before he left,' said Mercedes. 'Mr. Porsen goes up on to the hill every evening about an hour before dinner. It stimulates his mind. Paul knew he was on his way there and he had to go telling him how all the young men had to rock that stone to prove their courage. No one with any guts could have looked the damnable rock in the face and ignored it after that.'

'I could,' said Mandrake. 'But then I suppose I haven't any guts. Did anyone go with him?'

'No. He liked to be by himself when he went up there.'

'I see,' said Mandrake. 'Well, I'm supposed to be at the police station, but it seemed only reasonable to let you know on the way. I'm sorry to have brought such shocking news.'

'It was good of you to come,' said Bertrand. 'We had to know.'

When he was at the door Mandrake saw Hazel and stopped in his stride. He turned back across the room. 'I'd be glad if you'd walk a little way with me,' he said.

Hazel followed him out of the 'George.'

'Is there anything I can do?'

'Yes, possibly. Tell me if Porsen was really alone when he—fell.'

'I should think so,' said Hazel. 'We were all in the "George" when he left at about ten-past five. He was by himself then.'

Mandrake's face lightened. 'So you were in the "George" too?'

'Yes. I had to get some details about a wedding.'

'Splendid. And like a sensible girl you've been in the "George" ever since?'

'Whatever do you take me for? I went back to the office and wrote up my notes. Then I did my face and came back at a quarter to seven. Elizabeth Brentbridge had asked me and Hallam to a party ages ago, only she'd forgotten all about it, so it wasn't a great success.'

Mandrake's face was sober, but he spoke casually. 'Whom did you see at your office?'

'I don't think I actually saw anyone. Our room was empty when I came back. I wrote up my stuff and put it on Mr. Lightbody's table. He wasn't in his room, though. One of the girls was in the front office but I'm not sure who.'

'Did you leave the office open then?'

'No, I locked up. We've all got keys. The last one out on Saturdays always locks up. I stayed on because there wasn't time to get home and back for the party.'

'What a pity.'

'Whatever do you mean?'

'If anyone had been with Porsen when he fell off that rock the sensible thing would be to go straight to the police and say so—even if it were a bit embarrassing.'

'I suppose it would. Was anyone with him?'

Instead of answering Mandrake put his hand in his pocket. 'Can you tell me if there's anything special about this plant?' He drew out a sprig of yarrow.

'Why?'

'There was a small, freshly-pulled pile beside the Toad.'

Hazel felt hot and sick and ran her fingernails into her palms to get a grip on herself. Other people pulled yarrow out of lawns and gardens but only Paul, so far as she knew, pulled it out of pastures and commons automatically for no reason. Paul had left the 'George' a little after Lars and there had been earth on his fingers when he returned.

'It's a herb that is held by the old wives hereabouts to be good for the kidneys,' she wildly improvised. 'The children collect it.'

He watched her closely. 'You don't collect it yourself?'

'What do you mean?'

'I found this in the same place.'

He brought out his handkerchief and unfolded it. Between its folds was the partly-used book of matches, with 'HAZEL' neatly lettered on the cover. They were the matches she had given to Paul a few moments before he had left the 'George.'

Hazel said, 'I see,' and her colour began to come back. Even if Paul had dropped the matches near the Toad, Mandrake couldn't know that. He only thought he had found something that implicated Hazel. Paul hadn't entered his mind. It was up to her to handle things so that he never did.

Hazel said, 'Somebody wrote my name on a folder of book matches. It could have been Lars. He thought it was an unusual name. He might have wanted to remember it to use sometime in a picture. It might have been anyone, simply doodling. The girls in our office write names for minutes together, adding up the letters to see if they come to lucky numbers. And somebody pulled out a few weeds in an idle moment. That could have been Lars too, for that matter, or anyone. Why are you telling me?'

Mandrake shrugged his vast, shapeless shoulders. 'Sheer weakness of character,' he said. 'I don't for a moment suppose you pushed the man off the rock, but I thought if you had got yourself involved in any way you might decide to ask me not to mention these findings to the police, or else to come along with me and explain them. I'm on my way there now, you know.'

Hazel thought wildly. Supposing she were to tell the police she had been with Lars at the Rock and seen him fall—obviously nobody was likely to imagine she'd pushed him off, but was anyone in a position to call her bluff? She had told Mandrake she had established no alibi at her office. Now she remembered that, while she was alone there, Head Office had rung through twice and she had answered. They would know she couldn't have possibly got to the rock and back in between. Would anyone remember she had lent the matches to Paul? Who had been with them at the time? Mercedes, of course, Mercedes whose continuity-trained eye never missed anything, and who had made some sort of joke about cheap lighters. Mercedes would remember. And there could be finger-prints on the smooth cardboard. There could be soil under fingernails that matched the soil near the Toad. No, the police mustn't know about the matches.

Hazel felt icy cold. Too late to wonder if Mandrake was the kindly human being he sometimes seemed or a calculating, steel-hard intellect. If it was a trap that he had laid for her it was a trap, but she took her chance and Paul's. 'For pity's sake,' she said, 'don't tell the police.'

6

'I,' said the Fly, 'with my little eye.
I saw him die.'

T HEY were outside the police station. Mandrake
stood still with his foot on the step and regarded
Hazel seemingly from a great way off. Hazel took
a breath and firmly closed her mouth.

'Hadn't you better tell me a little more?'

'I can't. I can't tell anyone. Those are my matches.
Please don't say anything about them.'

'You know how he died?'

'No.'

'You were there. You saw him?' The words cracked
like pistol shots.

'I wasn't. I didn't.'

'Then why,' his voice was suddenly and almost
soothingly a whisper, 'why in the world not let them
have all the facts and work it out for themselves?'

'Because you promised . . .'

'I promised nothing.'

'No, of course you didn't. You merely and very
cleverly worded your suggestion so as to trap any
normally trusting person into assuming you intended a

promise and giving themselves away.' Her eyes were blazing. 'Go ahead and tell them, Professor,' she said bitterly.

The police sergeant was coming down the steps. 'Ah, it is Professor Mandrake, isn't it?' he said. 'We're waiting for you now in my office.' He stood aside for Mandrake to precede him. Hazel watched Mandrake desperately. For a long, silent moment he seemed to be lost in abstract calculations. At last he said:

'Good-bye, Hazel. It does seem a pity that such a lot had to happen on such a *matchless* evening, doesn't it?' He gave her a wicked smile. 'I mustn't keep the inspector waiting. You do understand, don't you?'

Hazel understood. She watched him follow the sergeant into the station, then turned and, with her breath coming in little gusts, almost ran along the street. Her bicycle was at the office. There was a light in the 'Junior Reporters',' and to her surprise she saw Beasley bent over the telephone. Her first thought was that something had gone wrong at home and he was 'phoning the hospital. Then she heard him saying, 'No, Lars. L for London, A for ambulance, R for Ronald, S for son . . . that's right, Lars Porsen . . .'

Somehow or other, even in the middle of becoming a father, Beasley had stumbled on the news story and was telephoning the London papers while it was 'hot.' Hazel opened the door. 'Don't interrupt,' said Beasley, 'I'm through to the news desk. Accident?' he went on into the telephone. 'Nobody knows. Could be any-thing. . . .'

Hazel knew what she must do. She took a deliberately

false step, lost balance, and fell heavily and painfully on top of the table, knocking the telephone sideways off the table on to the floor.

'Oh damn,' said Beasley, 'you've cut me off in the middle of the biggest news story of the year.' He picked up the receiver and put it to his ear. 'I'm cut off,' he said furiously.

Hazel climbed off the floor and put her hand over the microphone. 'Don't,' she said breathlessly. 'They'll wait. It's a better story than you know. I've just left Mandrake who found the body.'

Beasley softened a little. 'What's he got to say?'

'What do you know already? How did you hear?'

'I heard the ambulance bell going past our house. I ran out, but of course it had passed by then. I asked someone in the street and he said he thought it was one of the film people so I went to the "George" and they told me.'

'Told you what?'

'That Lars Porsen had been found dead up on the Down.'

'Is that all?'

'Isn't it enough? The director of Pegasus Pictures found dead without a clue as to how or why bang in the middle of making a picture? It could be murder. It could be anything. If that isn't an exclusive news story, nothing is. I'm going to 'phone it through to every Sunday paper in the country if I have to stay up till morning.'

Hazel knew suddenly that this was a story she had to handle even if it meant knocking out Beasley with a bottle and sitting on his head all night. No version of the fatality but her own must be allowed to sweep the country next morning. Beasley would plainly clutch at any straw or invent straws to make the story more sensational. An accidental death was nothing like such red meat as a mysterious one.

'Is everything all right at home?' she asked.

'Well—oh, yes. The baby's come. It's a boy.'

'Splendid. Is your wife all right?'

'Oh, she's a bit exhausted, you know, but pleased.'

'Don't you want to be there?'

'Well naturally, but I daren't miss a chance like this. She wouldn't want it.'

'I bet she would. I'll stay and send the story.'

'Would you? Oh, but you can't. It's late and I want to send it everywhere. I don't care how long it takes me.'

'Nor do I. I'll send it everywhere. I promise. You get back to Mrs. Beasley with my love.'

'But—I don't want to fall down on this . . .'

'Give me your notes and the name of every paper you want 'phoned. I won't fall down.'

At last she was alone and began to rewrite the story. For once she was sure that the persons taking down at the other end of the telephone would hear her out with patience, so she spread herself a little, dwelling on the director's 'playboy' characteristics and high-lighting the fact that he never refused a dare and was a child at heart before mentioning that, prior to the accident, he had taken a marked interest in a discussion about the Toad Rock, and had learned that the local girls dared their admirers to ride it and prove their courage.

She faithfully telephoned every paper on Beasley's list. Hazel's story might not be the whole truth, but she was going to get it in first. It would be on every breakfast table in the country next morning. Not for a moment should anyone be left to conjecture about the possible causes of a mysterious and violent death. A nation-wide suspicion or even curiosity would be far more likely to stir the police to closer investigation than a nation-wide acceptance of the thing as an accident. Hazel's story was designed to allay suspicion even before it was awakened.

As she telephoned Hazel began to wonder which paper Angela would read and whether it would come to her then with the first shock, or if someone from the unit would have spoken to her first on the telephone or sent her a wire, and whether she would be shaken or numb or secretly glad when the shock had begun to abate. Then she began to wonder if Lars had a mother; someone who had to love him whether he pulled the wings off butterflies or not, to grieve for the tumbled curls and melting brown eyes of the little boy Lars must have been. At this thought she inserted the word 'lovable' in the description of the director she was at that moment dictating in a voice that began to croak with the strain and had yet some calls to make.

But then she began to be haunted by another hypothetical mother with another heart to be broken and to visualize another small boy growing up in a difficult world. Paul at his prep school, Paul falling in love at his first grown-up theatre and, like Campion's Unhappy Shadow, following his fair sun to inevitable disaster.

But that, of course, was nonsense, a figment only of her brain, disordered by tension and lack of sleep. Paul could not, of course, kill anyone. There had been an accident to the man he happened to dislike and that was all. Only how had the matches that had been in Paul's hand when he left the 'George' got on to the scene of the accident unless Paul were there? Well, easily, Hazel argued with herself, for after all, they had been in *her* hand a few moments before that, and *she* hadn't been at the rock when Lars fell off. Only she knew where she had been and she didn't know where Paul had been. He'd left the 'George' and he hadn't returned till after Lars must have died. Suppose he'd gone after Lars and talked him into swinging on the rock—even challenged him by swinging on it himself first—and Lars had slipped? That wouldn't have been murder, but he might have preferred to say nothing about his share in it. It wouldn't have been murder, but somehow Hazel preferred to think that Paul had pushed his boss off the cliff in a clean, cold-blooded rage with the desperate intention of freeing his love from her union with a despicable cad. You could love a man who was prepared to kill for his lady. You could even be jealous of the lady so fanatically beloved. Hazel was.

It was almost daybreak and beginning to rain before Hazel locked the office and tottered out into the cold air. She could not help feeling furtive as she passed the police station, but no one appeared and the little town was deserted. As she started up the hill the rain became a steady downpour which quickly soaked her thin summer dress. The half-awake feeling that nothing that had happened could possibly be real and that soon she must wake up was quite dispelled by her physical wretchedness. This was reality all right, and if she awoke any further it would doubtless be to something worse. For one thing, however neatly she had tied up the press story, Mandrake was hardly likely to let things rest there. He might have betrayed her already to the police, though she felt sure he had not meant to do that. No, he would talk to her first and she must have her story ready—and it had better be convincing.

She could tell him that she had actually started home when she left the 'George' the first time, had sat down to rest near the Toad, lit a cigarette, dropped the matches, pulled a few weeds and gone home, never looking over the cliffside to learn that Lars lay there all the time. But if that had been true what had been the need to hide it when he first asked her—why had she said she'd really been at the office? No, the story must be a little shameful to account for her reluctance to admit it in the first place. Naturally the obvious story was the best one if only Hazel could tell it convincingly, that she had met Lars by accident or by appointment on her way up the hill, had gone for an unsavoury little jaunt in his car, had sat on the grass by the Toad with him and that, to impress her, he had ridden the Toad and slipped off to his death.

If she could tell that story and stick to it everything was neat as could be. But she was such an unpractised liar that she distrusted her power to convince Mandrake. After all, she reasoned, as the rain seeped through to her skin, she did not actually have to *tell* him this story, only to deny it in an unconvincing way, for the story was exactly what anyone knowing Lars would guess at, and surely to say, 'Oh no, he never, really; I wouldn't let him. I'm not that sort of girl. We were only kidding . . . I told him to be careful not to slip . . .' was not beyond her powers. Of course, if Mandrake decided to take that much to the police she would have to come out into the open and be more explicit, but by that time no doubt she would have got used to the part. And surely it was better that she should cut a slightly sorry figure in her home town than that Paul should cease to cut any sort of figure at all for ever and for ever and for ever. Besides, and a sudden quickening of her blood warmed her numbed body a little, if she were forced into making a public statement Paul, at least, would know it was false; and he would know why.

She put her bicycle in the shed and let herself in with her key, squelching upstairs as silently as was possible. As she peeled off her clothes she noticed a tray with sandwiches and a thermos of cocoa. Presently the door opened and her mother came in with a bath towel.

'Sorry, Mum. Were you worried?'

'A bit. Are you all right? I'll rub your feet.'

'Yes. I'm all right. There was a story I had to 'phone to the London papers. I couldn't let you know.'

'I told your father it's time we got the 'phone up here. They oughtn't to keep you all night though.'

'It was my own fault, really. A man got killed. That film director. He fell off the Toad Rock and it had to be sent to all the Sunday papers.'

'Did it? It doesn't seem healthy to get paid for that sort of thing.'

'It's all right, Mum. I shan't be paid. You see I was really on my way home when I found Mr. Beasley starting to send it. He needs the money, but his wife's just got her baby. I told him to go home and I'd do it. It was my fault, you see, but I put his name to the stories. He'll get the money.'

'Wouldn't it have done on Monday?'

'No. It would be stale by then.'

'I see. Go to sleep then, pet, and don't try to get up in the morning. I'll bring you some lunch when you wake. Go to sleep now.'

Hazel pushed her legs down the bed and pulled the blankets round her shoulders and the waking nightmare gave place to the sleeping one in which Lars' mother and Mercedes, Angela Wingless and Mandrake were dancing ring-a-roses with Hazel round the Toad Rock, upon which Paul was rocking savagely with Beasley's baby in his arms. With each swing back of the rock, blood gushed from underneath it. Hazel kept trying to break out of the wildly dancing circle, to stand in front of the rock so that no one else should see the blood, but Mandrake had one of her hands in a grip of iron and Mercedes had an equally relentless grasp on the other. At last Hazel broke free to find that it was not blood at all but her lost magenta lipstick, crushed under the rocking stone.

When at last she waked the rain had stopped, the sun was high in the sky and the nightmare had vanished wholly from her mind. It was quite a while before she even remembered about Lars or her affairs of the previous night, and even longer before she actually believed them. She got out of bed and stretched and almost immediately her mother came in with a tray. Hazel smiled and hugged her. A mother was something extraordinarily solid to hold on to in the middle of a tottering world.

'It's a lovely day after the rain,' said Mrs. Fairweather. 'Your father's so pleased about the garden. He's been wanting it for days. And such a nice man has looked over the gate and admired it, an artist. He was talking to your father for ten minutes about it. Said it's the sort of typical English garden you never see nowadays. He asked if he could make some sketches and your father insisted on him staying to lunch. They're getting on like a house on fire. He's there on the lawn, now.'

Hazel moved across the room to the little window and drew back the lilac-sprigged curtain. There, like the rock of ages, with an expression of concentrated happiness on his face, sat Mandrake at his easel in the middle of the lawn.

The flavour had gone out of Hazel's meal before she touched it but she did her best to eat. Then she dressed and came downstairs with the desperate intention of slipping out and going for a walk, but her father pounced on her instantly and introduced her to Mandrake.

'We've met before,' said Hazel rather coldly, 'several times.'

'Why, so we have,' replied Mandrake cordially. 'What a strange coincidence.'

'The actual expression is, "it's a small world," ' said Hazel. 'I've got rather a headache, Dad. I think I'll go for a walk.'

'Oh, don't do that,' said Mr. Fairweather. 'It would be rather rude to our visitor. You can get just as much fresh air in the garden.'

Hazel gave in.

'Why not do a bit of weeding if you're at a loose end?' suggested her father. 'It's wonderfully relaxing.'

'It doesn't relax me,' said Hazel gracelessly.

'It did last Sunday though,' said her father mildly, spraying D.D.T. lotion over the greenfly on the roses. 'When that young man was here. He was a really keen gardener, wasn't he? Never known a keener. Weeded the lawn almost clear of yarrow in one afternoon. What was his name . . .?'

'He weeded the dandelions as well,' said Hazel rather pointlessly, and regretted it at once.

'Oh no. Never touched anything but yarrow,' insisted her father. 'He said he was a specialist and could only tackle one thing at a time. It was yarrow or nothing. It fascinated him the way the roots ran under the grass and kept popping up in another place, one always leading to another. He said it worked like madness in the brain. I suppose it could, too.'

Hazel prayed that it might not work at all in Mandrake's but the professor had his vast back to her and was tenderly dotting in the eye of a daisy with a brushful of cadmium yellow. 'It's left a lot of bare patches on the lawn,' she replied discouragingly.

'Ah, you can't make an omelette without breaking

eggs,' said Fairweather. 'A lawn is the work of a life-time. I shall resow the patches in the autumn.' He moved on to the potting shed some way down the garden. Hazel dropped on the grass beside Mandrake. 'Did you know I lived here?' she asked under her breath.

'I spoke to your editor on the telephone. A most obliging man.'

'I suppose I should have expected you,' said Hazel. 'But I'd rather not talk to you here. Do I have to?'

Her carefully thought out rôle of giggling slyness was going to suffer sadly under her parents' eyes.

'Your mother is in the house preparing tea. Your father is totally absorbed in the process of dissolving his second packet of Sluggicide in two gallons of tepid water. He read me all the instructions off the packet. Relax and tell me the truth.'

'I can't do both at once,' said Hazel, and then realized she was out of character. She tried again. 'Well, anyway, I did tell you the truth.'

'That you were not there when the accident happened? Then who was there?'

Hazel plucked a grass stalk. 'Those things that you found don't prove that anyone was there *when it happened*.'

'Perhaps not, but someone was there.'

'How can you know that?'

'Through my observations of the man's character, observations only partly borne out by the Sunday newspapers, for while they refer to him as a playboy who could never refuse a dare . . .'

'Do they?' asked Hazel in gratified tones, for she had not yet seen any papers.

'They do. But I should suppose him capable of refusing any dare unless there were somebody watching. . . .'

Mrs. Fairweather came out from the house with a newspaper in her hand. 'Look, darling,' she said, 'I hadn't remembered to look at the paper till now. They've put your story in and it looks very nice.' She spread the pages on the grass in front of them. 'My daughter's a journalist, you know.' She beamed maternally. 'Last night she was kept at the office nearly till daybreak, sending an important story through to all the London papers. She handled it all by herself.'

'How very interesting,' said Mandrake. 'What a gifted young woman your daughter must be.'

'Well, of course, I think so,' said Mrs. Fairweather with temperate pride, 'but then. I'll have tea ready in a jiffy. I'm making a few scones.'

She retired into the house.

'Well, well,' said Mandrake quietly. 'What a singularly thorough young woman. You sat up all night propagating a version of the event that couldn't leave a shadow of doubt in anyone's mind. You've even anticipated the coroner's verdict of accidental death. You could have reported the death and left the cause to be determined, but no, you went further. Now why?'

'I had to make the best of my material . . .'

'Then you would have left a reasonable doubt. A slight mystery would have made far more sensational reading.'

'And the London papers would have sent reporters and the local police have been on their toes—and then maybe you would have told someone that I was there at the time.'

'But you say you weren't.'

'And you don't believe me.'

'I know someone was there.'

'How?'

'I've told you. *If* Lars ever rocked on the Toad at all he had an audience. . . .'

'*If!* But of course he did.'

'How can you know unless you were there? If he *didn't* meet his end by slipping off the Toad in front of an impressed lady, he didn't meet his end by accident—in which event he must have been pushed. There's got to be a witness or a murderer.'

'Well, all right.' Hazel turned her face away from him. 'Suppose I did get in the car when he suggested a little run, there wasn't any harm in that, was there?'

'Not so far.'

'When he stopped by the Toad *I* didn't suggest he should rock it. I tried to persuade him not to. Someone was killed there once before . . .'

'I know. It said so in my newspaper.'

'Well, when he went over I felt dreadful. I looked over the edge and when I realized he was dead I just panicked and ran down the hill as fast as I could. You wouldn't really expect me to tell anyone if I could help it, would you?'

'Not really.'

'And now what have you got, anyway? The same

story that was in the papers. Nothing to add to it except that I was there. Is that worth making a song about? If it's worth your while to drag that out of me at the inquest just to gratify your passion for amateur detection, go ahead.'

'Now you've hurt my feelings,' said Mandrake. 'The truth is that besides knowing somebody was there I am equally certain it couldn't have been you. And I think you know who it was.'

'How can you know it wasn't I?'

'When I found the body my first action was to loosen the tie in case he wasn't quite dead. It was tied with a left-handed knot.'

'Perhaps Lars was left-handed.'

'He wasn't.'

'What difference does it make?'

'Normally you tie the knot in the wide flap and tighten it by sliding the knot up the narrow end which runs round the left side of the neck. Lars' tie was tied the other way, with the narrow end coming round the right side of his neck.'

'And that suggests . . .?' inquired Hazel coolly, though her heart was beginning to thump with terror and she kept her face away from him. If she didn't keep her wits about her now she would be stampeded into admitting she hadn't been there and this man would bore on like a road-drill till she'd told him all she knew.

'It suggests that his tie was off when he died and that it was tied on by somebody else.'

'Does it suggest why he took it off?'

'I have given the matter some thought. You might

take off your tie to fight someone or because you were going to sleep. If you were in a fight you might be killed. You might be strangled in your sleep and rolled over a cliff. But the person who killed you wouldn't leave the tie lying about if he wanted it to look like an accident. He'd tie it round the dead man's collar before he rolled him over the cliff; at least I would, if I kept my nerve. And when you tie a tie on somebody else you tie it the other way. Now I can think of no circumstances in which *you* would be likely to tie a tie round a dead man's collar. So honestly I don't think you were there. But someone was.'

'Yes, someone was. You've only thought of two reasons for a man to take off his tie on a hot day. I could supply another. Suppose he wanted to relax and—dally—with the lady. Quite a number of men feel more comfortable without their ties. Suppose the—lady—to have been in a mood for dalliance . . .' Hazel's head was turned from Mandrake so he could not see the distaste on her face, 'and, afterwards, suppose she tied his tie on again all in the playful spirit of the moment.'

'I find it hard to suppose.'

'I'm not finding it easy to tell you.'

Mandrake's gaze suddenly sharpened and he grasped her shoulders so that she had to look him in the face. 'And his collar? Am I to suppose that she also replaced the back stud in his collar on his pudgy little neck in the same idyllic spirit.'

Hazel shut her eyes. 'He was wearing a fixed collar,' she guessed desperately, for she had not the slightest recollection what type of shirt Lars wore. Mandrake looked depressed. Then he rallied. 'And you are telling me that *after that* he pranced upon the rock? After he had, if I don't mistake you, bent the lady to his will? Surely it was hardly necessary to prove his manhood then?'

Hazel replied in a lifeless whisper. 'He was highly exhilarated.'

A silence fell between them, heavy with the drone of bees and an occasional distant squelch from Mr. Fairweather's pest-killing excursion. At last Mandrake said 'And is that the story you would tell if you were confronted by the police?'

'In the face of your evidence I should have no choice,' replied Hazel distinctly. '*You* are the only one with a choice. If you speak up you will be proved a formidable detective; I shall be humiliated without mercy and the course of justice will not be advanced one jot.'

'On the contrary, the course of justice will be positively impeded by your fantastic human sacrifice,' said Mandrake. 'You have made your point. The police must be left out.'

The relief on Hazel's face faded to a look of apprehension. 'What do you mean?' she said. 'Out of what?'

'Your story is perfect and accounts for everything. It's a work of art in every particular but one.'

'What is that?'

'Character—your character.'

'Test it in any way you like. I shan't waver from my account.'

'That's just what I mean. The lady in your version is

a lady who wavered at every turn. And now,' he appeared to dismiss the whole business and turned back with enthusiasm to his easel, 'my picture is almost completed, but I feel it lacks some accent in this lower corner. It appears that, in spite of the keen pursuit of the young man—whoever he was—who was here last Sunday, there lingers one spray of yarrow here at the edge of the grass, and that, with your permission, I shall add.'

But Hazel was not playing mouse to his cat any longer. 'I should,' she agreed. 'And you haven't put in any greenfly either. You're missing lots of opportunities. I think I'll go in and help Mummy with tea.'

Before she could reach the house, however, she heard the click of the garden gate and turned, frozen, in the porch. With the pleased expression of one perfectly sure of his welcome, Paul was walking up the path.

7

*That's a parenthesis. The very name
of 'garden' really carries one astray.*

ANTHONY C. DEANE

AZEL's heart turned over. Of all the occasions when he might have come, why must he arrive at that moment to drop into Mandrake's plan like the last piece in the jigsaw? Paul would start to weed and then Mandrake would know—if he hadn't guessed already. No, at any cost he must be prevented.

'Hullo,' said Paul. 'Can I come to tea?'

With desperate entreaty in her eyes, Hazel went to meet him, still trying to decide what to do. Mandrake was much too close for her to warn him. Paul took both her hands. 'You remind me of a peak in Darien,' he said.

'Was I looking at you with a wild surmise? How embarrassing for you.' She drew her hands from his, put them round his neck, pressed her cheek to his and with her lips touching his ear whispered soundlessly, 'Don't weed.'

It was the fresh, soft touch of a child or a kitten and

Paul's long arms had wrapped themselves round her before the rest of him was aware of the contact. Across her head he saw Mandrake pretending not to watch them over the top of his easel and, not being a conceited man, he put two and two together and arrived at a totally wrong conclusion. This extraordinary man had been bothering the child again and she wanted Paul to act as some sort of buffer and not to become so absorbed in weeding that he left her unprotected. It was a charming big-brotherly rôle, and in pursuance of it he kissed her very lightly on the top of the head.

Hazel twisted out of his arms. 'This is Professor Mandrake,' she said. 'He's painting the lilies.'

'There aren't any lilies,' said Mandrake. 'How do you do?'

'But we've met already,' said Paul, crossing to the easel in a few strides. 'You're staying at the "George" and it was you who—who——'

'It was I who found the body,' agreed Mandrake.

'Oh yes,' said Hazel, still trying to warn Paul, 'and he couldn't have liked it more. The Professor is fascinated by bodies . . . and clues and everything like that.'

'Clues,' said Paul, stretching himself on the grass between them. 'Clues to what?'

'Well naturally, to murder.'

'But no one has suggested murder.'

'That's the frustrating part,' explained Hazel. 'From the Professor's point of view it's such a waste.'

Mandrake deepened a shadow on the underside of a leaf with a little Viridian. 'Nature has already made a buffoon of me,' he said with dignity. 'Your mockery is superfluous.'

Hazel regarded him levelly. 'You really shouldn't play for sympathy at this stage,' she said.

'No,' admitted Mandrake. 'I really shouldn't.' He put down his brushes and leaned towards Paul. 'But frankly,' he said in a confidingly man-to-man voice, 'laying all sentiment aside, don't you feel it's a pity it had to be plain accident? Here we have the sudden and violent death of a man for whom surely nobody will weep. Think how we could have whiled away the drowsy afternoons working out suspects and motives and alibis.'

'There's nothing to prevent you doing that,' said Paul accommodatingly. 'Let's pick ourselves some suspects. Is there any one you fancy?'

Mandrake did not answer, being busy trying to scrub out some Cerulean that had seeped over the edges of a ladybird. Paul's hand stole absently towards the sole sprig of yarrow within view but Hazel was too quick for him. Her fingers pounced and held his in a tense but trembling grasp. Clutching his hand as though her life depended on it, while a blush seemed to rise from her fingers and end at her ears, she began to talk breathlessly.

'Professor Mandrake is my fancy. After all, he found the body. He must have been there. He's the only one in the world who doesn't need an alibi.'

'He'd need a motive though, wouldn't he?' asked Paul, changing his hold on her fingers to a rather more comfortable one without letting go.

'He's got a motive,' said Hazel. 'Adventure. He's a born amateur. That means he does things, not for gain or for necessity but for love. And he loves crime.'

'Good heavens,' said Mandrake in a shocked and rather delighted voice. 'Go on.'

'He did it,' continued Hazel, 'for the pure excitement of getting away with a murder and now he finds he's done it too well. It's been accepted as accident. That's no good to him at all. Murderers are notoriously conceited. He wanted this to go down in history as the clueless murder, the work of a master mind. He wants to hear it talked about and to sit chuckling at what he knows. But nobody will talk about it. That's why *he* brings it into the conversation all the time.'

Hazel's fingers were growing quite at ease in Paul's reassuring grip. Perhaps one day she would have an opportunity to explain that she hadn't intended throwing herself at his head but at least it was comforting that he didn't offer any objection.

Mandrake was considering Hazel's theory with grave detachment. 'Yes,' he admitted, 'you have certainly improvized the sort of motive that would lift the crime out of the pedestrian rut into which most crimes fall and that is where your theory deviates from real life. Real life always lets us down with the motive. However imaginative a crime may appear at the outset, the motive is always a disappointment. It is always dull.'

'Perhaps crime doesn't attract the best brains,' suggested Paul.

'One is forced to that conclusion,' admitted

Mandrake. 'And yet many quite excellent brains are attracted by its solution.'

'Your own, for instance?' said Hazel.

'My own among others,' replied Mandrake. 'And always there is this element of anti-climax in the motive. Now I, were I to kill, should do it for the purely academic experience of pitting my brain against some of the best brains in the country and getting away with it. Hazel would kill for love. We'll grant her that. Why would you kill?'

The mild blue eyes with their air of detached speculation fastened their gaze on Paul's face. Paul didn't look up. 'If I were in danger, I suppose, or if someone I loved were in danger,' he replied after a moment.

'There are so many degrees of danger,' said Mandrake, 'and so many degrees of love. Mother love, yes, that would certainly kill if called upon to do so, and a man or a woman might kill for their actual mate—but love in the abstract, now, would anyone kill for an ideal that mightn't even exist?'

His gaze, though still benign, was fixed unwaveringly on Paul.

'Yes, of course,' said Paul. 'It's what we all had to do during the war.'

'The war,' said Mandrake. 'Ah yes, that must have made it very bothering afterwards to adapt oneself to conditions in which violence was—not in order.'

'Very bothering indeed,' agreed Paul. 'One is constantly encountering circumstances in which it has caused no end of bother. Either life is sacred or it isn't. We've been taught that it isn't.'

138

Hazel's mother appeared in the doorway with the tea-tray. Paul got to his feet to help her and Mrs. Fairweather greeted him with delight. Together they laid the tea-things on a green-painted table in the shade while Hazel summoned her father and fetched another cup.

As the acknowledgment of the excellence of Mrs. Fairweather's scones and their consumption replaced conversation, Hazel tried to foresee Mandrake's next move. If only he would go to wash his hands and give her a moment in which to warn Paul; but he had already refused her most pressing invitation to do so. How could she warn Paul in any case without letting him know she supposed him to have killed Lars? If he had killed Lars he might be considerably irritated; if he hadn't he might justifiably be even more annoyed. How much did Mandrake guess, she was wondering, while she pressed more scones and far more butter than was reasonable on him. He must guess that she was shielding someone, and he knew, for she had told him a week ago, that she was in love with Paul. So far he didn't know that Paul had ever possessed a packet of matches with 'Hazel' written on the cover, nor that he was the young man who had been so keen a weeder of yarrow. But as Paul had no idea of the importance of these trifles he might easily give them away. Back of the feverish workings of her mind was the unnerving discovery that the man she loved could kill a man and still be the man she loved.

Mandrake asked if he might smoke. Paul offered his packet and Mandrake took one and thanked him, then pretended to hunt for a match. Hazel was sure he didn't smoke but was trying to find out if Paul habitually used a lighter or matches and prayed that Paul would produce his lighter and that it would work, but her father was first with a match. Mandrake was left puffing irritably at his cigarette and coughing a little.

He tried again. 'Your daughter thinks I killed the film director,' he said mildly and conversationally to Mrs. Fairweather.

Mrs. Fairweather looked startled. 'There you are,' said Hazel. 'He's done it again.'

'Done what again?' asked Mr. Fairweather in some embarrassment.

'Brought the body into the conversation.'

'But she can't really think you killed him, Professor Mandrake,' protested Mrs. Fairweather. 'She surely didn't say so, did she, not to a guest?'

'She did. She's built up quite a case against me.'

'Oh, Hazel. You must apologize at once. She's not very well to-day, Professor. She walked home last night in all that rain and got soaked to the skin. Why, whoever would want to kill a man like that?'

'I suppose there's always someone liable to gain by anyone's death,' suggested Mr. Fairweather.

'Well, no one in the film company,' said Hazel. 'They'd all be out of work, wouldn't they?'

'Would they?' said Mandrake to Paul.

'I couldn't be sure, offhand,' said Paul. 'It's never happened to me in a picture before. I suppose it all depends whether Head Office decides to scrap the picture or to send down a new director—and on what contracts people have got. In any case, it won't have done the picture any good, and artists and technicians are only as good as the picture they've made. I don't think anyone in the unit will have welcomed his death.'

'No sane man welcomes anybody's death,' said Mandrake.

'Except you,' whispered Hazel in a voice that she hoped her parents wouldn't hear.

'My sanity, like everyone else's, balances on a hair-spring,' replied Mandrake without rancour. 'What I am trying to say is that there is no sane motive for murder. Therefore we need not look for a sane motive.'

'And you don't have to look for a motive at all when the thing was an obvious accident,' said Mrs. Fair-weather flatly. 'It's morbid and unnatural and I don't know how Hazel got started on it. The man was a proper little show-off as everyone knew and that rock has been a positive menace to show-offs ever since I was a girl.'

'You don't show off to *no one*,' said Mandrake doggedly.

'*He* might have,' said Mrs. Fairweather, clearly having borne with quite enough of this conversation in her domain. 'Not being sure of his powers he might have practised by himself to make sure of being able to show off when there *was* someone there.'

With an air that suggested there need be no further nonsense she got to her feet, took the tray and departed into the house. Paul picked up the tea-pot and hot-water jug and followed. Hazel looked sideways at Mandrake.

'Your mother has made quite a point there,' he

admitted. 'I must say the Fairweather women hang together.'

'The Fairweather women,' said Hazel, 'practically never hang. That cigarette's got all twisted, Professor. Do let me give you a new one—and a match.'

'No thank you,' said Mandrake crossly, stubbing the soggy thing into his saucer. Hazel put the saucer and its cup into one of his hands and the honey-pot into the other. 'In there,' she directed. 'Down the passage and on the right.' She smiled. 'It's considered to be the least one can do.'

Mandrake moved with his burden towards the porch where he met Paul coming out. 'Come and show me the way to the kitchen,' he pleaded, but Paul assured him he couldn't miss it and came back to the table where Hazel was folding the cloth. Mr. Fairweather arose and wandered back towards the slugs.

Paul said, 'There's something wrong, isn't there? Has Mandrake been bothering you?'

'Not exactly—at least—not me, but I've got to talk to you . . .' But Mandrake had disposed of his task and was ambling back to them with astonishing haste.

'I'm going to help with the washing-up,' said Hazel.

'I'll come too,' said Paul.

'So will I,' said Mandrake. 'I feel sure it's the least I can do.'

'Three drying to one washing-up is too many,' protested Hazel. 'It'll put mother off her stroke.'

'I should like to meet your mother when she's off her stroke,' said Mandrake, plodding resolutely back into the kitchen.

But it was Hazel who was off her stroke. Once when she and Paul reached for the same plate she felt the singeing contact of his fingers and let go the plate so that it was smashed. Mandrake stood a moment regarding Hazel, then he said in a quite changed voice, 'Madam, do you happen to have a thermometer in the house?'

Mrs. Fairweather turned and looked at him and then at her daughter. Hazel's face was flushed and her teeth were chattering a little. Mrs. Fairweather dried her hands and placed one on Hazel's forehead. It was hot and throbbing.

Within ten minutes Hazel had been firmly tucked into bed and had even given up protesting. She felt almost grateful for the cool pillow below her hot cheek and the hot bottle below her surprisingly cold feet. Her mother departed and presently came back.

'They've gone off together,' she said.

'Professor Mandrake hadn't finished his painting.'

'He said he'd rather not finish it at one sitting; it would give him an excuse to come again.' Mrs. Fairweather looked fleetingly gratified but added, 'I shall have to put him on to margarine though.'

'And Paul?'

'He seemed very worried because he wouldn't be able to telephone you here. The Professor said never mind, they'd go down to the town and send you some flowers. I said they couldn't on a Sunday, and he said they'd do it first thing in the morning.'

'I shall be in the office first thing in the morning.'

'We'll see about that.'

'I must be in the office first thing in the morning. I've got to cover the inquest.'

'An inquest's no place for a young girl at the best of times.'

'It's part of my job.'

'Is it? I suppose it is. Whoever would have thought that writing nature poetry in your rough note-book would end up like this?'

'I don't know,' said Hazel, 'but I've got to be at the inquest.'

HAZEL wasn't at the inquest. Mr. Lightbody
decided to 'cover' it himself. Always before
Hazel would have moved heaven and earth to
avoid an inquest but this time she hovered miserably
about the office, repeating that it would be valuable
experience for her. Mr. Lightbody remained uncon-
vinced and went alone. On his return he made no
mention of the verdict and Hazel was driven to offering
to type out his shorthand notes, but that, too, he
preferred to do himself.

She began to fear she would have to wait till the
Sallowshire Guardian came out on Friday and had
completed a description of the Old Timers' Carnival
Supper Dance when Lightbody, emerging from his
office to borrow a match from her, vouchsafed that it
had been a good inquest and that two London papers
had sent representatives.

'Are they going on with the film?' asked Hazel.

'I imagine so. As a matter of fact I asked one of the
unit and he referred me to their publicity man.'

'I didn't know there was one.'

'He came down to-day for the inquest, a Mr. Rupert Rollo. He asked me to lunch.' Mr. Lightbody stared for a longish time at the book-matches in his hand, with Hazel's name pencilled across them, then, with the same air of concentration, placed them in his pocket and went back into his office. He had done this so often before that Hazel felt no alarm. In fact, she felt hopeful that he could not have gazed so long and so detachedly at the matches if a similar packet had been mentioned by Mandrake in the evidence he had just been reporting. She was probably in the clear. Hazel fell to work on the description of the presentation of a silver cake-stand and biscuit barrel to Miss Levity, the retiring postmistress, with a better heart.

At three minutes to one the door swung open and a young man walked in and addressed her by name. He had fair hair brushed up at the temples, a nose that turned up the merest fraction, and a smile that even he must have regarded as irresistible.

'Miss Fairweather?' He sauntered across the office and sat on the corner of her table, balancing his cane and smiling roguishly.

'Yes?'

'My name's Rupert Rollo.'

'Oh. You want Mr. Lightbody?'

'No, if the truth were known, I don't.' The grin became confidential. 'I've *got* him, but it works out it's you I wanted, just between you and me and the gatepost.'

'He's just in there,' said Hazel.

'Oh-o. Thanks for the tip.' Mr. Rollo lowered his voice. 'Well, you probably know I'm Pegasus' Public Relations Officer, come down to get things under way again as soon as the verdict was out . . .'

'What was the verdict?'

'Good heavens, don't you know? Accident. Not as good as Natural Causes from my point of view, but good enough to let us get on with the job without interference. You see, we're all as full of human sympathy as the next man, but we can't afford to waste time. Lars Porsen may have been the best-hearted little blackguard in the business, but it doesn't alter the fact that all the artists and all the technicians are under contract and time is marching on, and they'll all expect to be paid one hundred per cent. per minute for any time off for decent grief and proper sentiment. So we've got to get right back to the business of making pictures. But it's got to look all right to the public and we need your co-operation.'

'Mine?'

'Well, press co-operation. I had a few words with Professor Mandrake after the inquest and he tells me it was you, not Lightbody, who handled the story for the Sunday papers.'

'Yes,' said Hazel.

'Then, you're the girl for our money. I couldn't have done it better myself.'

'I was told I'd missed all the possibilities.'

'Couldn't have been better from our point of view. You see we want to make the public feel that a director dropping down dead in the middle of a production is just one of those things that might happen in any picture but that the Show Goes On in spite of it. So you'll come along to lunch with me and I'll give you the layout for the next release, eh?'

'Well, but I can't promise that a word I may say will be printed in future. I only sent the first story through because I got left in the office when it happened. Mr. Lightbody is certain to handle it for our own district, and some of the London papers have sent representatives to the inquest. They're not likely to refer to me.'

'They're lunching with me too, so is the bank manager, the manager of the Co-op., the Chairman of the Rotarians and some of the unit.'

'And so is Mr. Lightbody.'

'And so are you, I hope. Even if you don't know your own strength, I'd like to have you on our side. Put on your bonnet,' persisted Mr. Rollo, 'or your false eyelashes and bosom or whatever it is you're liable to do before coming to lunch with a wolf like me.'

'Well, I could pumice-stone the ink off my fingers,' offered Hazel, not wishing to appear uncooperative.

Rollo put the two London reporters between Hazel and Mercedes, with Elizabeth opposite where they could look at her and where anything she might say could be quickly cancelled out by Mercedes or Hazel. During the earlier stages of the meal he did a wonderfully sustained piece of skating over thin ice, speaking warmly and sorrowfully of the late director but never letting the conversation rest on a note of depression or finality and never putting a foot wrong. At last he came to the point. The Show Must Go On. That was the tradition in British pictures, and it was a worth-while tradition, whatever the personal sorrow—sublimation could only be found in work and work and yet more work—and what more worth-while memorial could be found to the wholehearted genius of Lars Porsen than that this, his finest and most dedicated endeavour, should be carried forward to a triumphant conclusion, exactly as he would have wished? Indeed, they owed it to his memory that the show should go on. Meantime, however, as a tribute to his memory and a gesture of appreciation to the townsfolk for their sympathy, it had been suggested that Pegasus Pictures should take upon itself the public duty of removing the Toad Rock for ever so that never again in the history of mankind should a man or a youth full of promise be tempted to ride it to his doom. Rollo, it appeared, had personally been up and inspected this obvious menace to the nation's youth, before the inquest, and, if the towns-people were agreeable, Elizabeth Brentbridge herself had volunteered to put the necessary machinery in motion that would effect the destruction of the rock a little before sunset to-morrow evening.

The suggestion was well received; it had been a good lunch. The townsmen welcomed the offer and the press-men were observed to be making a note of the time and place. Seldom, thought Hazel, could the expenditure of a little dynamite be hoped to yield so rich a harvest in publicity and goodwill.

Towards the lower end of the table Orlando Hallam was leaning forward trying to be heard. At last he got

Rollo's attention. 'And the picture,' he inquired, pitching his voice on a shrill note in the hope of penetrating the conversation, 'do we understand that the picture will continue?'

'Of course.' Mr. Rollo tried not to show his irritation over the fact that the point of his really admirable speech should have slipped past the author and require to be made again. 'The show will go on. Pegasus Pictures have been fortunate in acquiring the services of Manfred Mantobar who is, in fact, the nephew of Simon Mantobar, one of our producers. He will be here this evening or, at latest, to-morrow. He will spend a couple of days familiarizing himself with the script, seeing rushes and conferring with personnel; after that it will be action stations; each man to his post, each ready to give of his best and more than his best in spite of this unusual but by no means unsurmountable set-back, in order to carry the picture through to a triumphant finish.'

Rollo was sweating a little by now, but his point was undeniably made.

'Oh, hell,' a whisper exploded like a cracker into the ensuing hush, 'I was afraid we'd get Manfred. We were asking for it.'

It was Bertrand's voice. Mercedes flashed him a look and he lapsed into silence again. Hazel looked at Mercedes. Her eyes were bright and feverish and her face greyish. Had Lars' death really cut her to the heart or had she merely left off some of her make-up out of deference? Was she the dog that would run to the new master and lick his hand or the dog that would crawl to the old master's grave and lie there, growling till she died of hunger? She looked round suddenly into Hazel's eyes and her gaze was so black and bitter that Hazel felt a shock almost of fear. She was a one-man dog, all right, and the man was dead. Heaven help her then, thought Hazel, and let's hope she's brilliant at her job. For no one was likely to engage her out of friendship or because she was a pleasant person to have around.

Conversation broke out generally and Hazel heard one of the pressmen saying to Rollo, 'Quite a stunt, this blowing up the Rock, eh?'

Rollo grinned. 'It's going to be something. Perfect setting, that rock and Elizabeth here, silhouetted against the naked sky. I've got Television O.B. Unit all lined up.'

'Television?' said the pressmen. 'Are they sending?'

'Sure, sure. It's just their stuff. G. B. may be sending too.'

'But how could you have known?'

'Well, you have to plan a bit in advance of events,' explained Rollo expansively. 'Of course I had to wait for the inquest, but I went over to the spot and heard all the known facts yesterday as soon as I arrived and it looked like a natural to me. She'll make a speech you know, won't you, honey?'

'Sure,' agreed Elizabeth, 'so long as you give it me in time. Will I want make-up?'

'Good lord, no,' said Rollo rather abruptly, and shifted the conversation out of Elizabeth's territory at once, but Hazel had a feeling that she would probably be made-up by the unit man when the time came. She

felt a little sick, too, but that might be attributed to the
unaccustomed richness of the meal for which, after all,
she was grateful.

Paul wasn't at the lunch party and she gathered he
hadn't been at the inquest. She wondered if he supposed her to be still in bed, but she scarcely even
wondered if he had actually sent her any flowers. The
sort of man who was likely to send flowers was almost
never the sort of man from whom you'd want them.
Mandrake might send flowers as he had suggested, not
Paul.

Back at the office she was told that Paul had telephoned for her, had learned she was back at work,
inquired after her health and had rung off with no
further message. It wasn't much, but it was enough to
redeem the day from total oblivion and she went off to
the Women's Institute exhibition of handicrafts with a
good heart.

It wasn't till fairly late next afternoon that she
managed to think up an excuse to get Lightbody to
send her to the Pegasus studio. It wasn't even a good
excuse, but things were slack in the office and he let her
go. She was to interview Manfred Mantobar, the new
director, and get his opinion, so long as it was flattering,
of Steeple Tottering.

The hangar seemed bleak, the atmosphere apathetic.
The few technicians appeared neither interested in her
arrival nor resentful of it. She wandered unmolested
through the workshops and out into the yard where she
could hear the whirring of the projector. Someone must
be seeing the rushes—probably Mantobar—she decided

and came back into the hangar to where a row of small doors marked off the improvized office section. She tapped on the first two doors and got no answer.

Then she tapped on the third which still bore Lars Porsen's name. 'Come in,' called Mercedes' voice, and Hazel opened the door.

'Hullo,' said Mercedes. 'Come in. I'm putting the house in order for Mantobar.'

'Is he here?' asked Hazel. 'I'm supposed to interview him.'

'Good heavens. Then you'd better have your mind made up about what you intend him to say and see that he says it. If you give him his head on a "Yes-No—or Don't Know" issue, you're lost. He *doesn't* know.'

'Is it as bad as that?'

'Manfred is the great white cipher of the British Film Industry. He's Simon's nephew, and so far Simon's usually managed to farm him out into other companies when they've owed him a bad debt or something. The fact that he's wished him on to us gives you a pretty clear idea what he thinks of the picture's chances.'

'Does it mean it will be a failure?'

'Not necessarily. Lars had everything pretty well lined up on paper. Gussie and Bert and Paul know their jobs. Manfred'll go through the motions and they'll get on with the work just the same. It happens oftener than you guess. Of course it won't be the same as if Lars had finished it, but the public'll come, anyway. They'll have to. We've got distribution.'

'What's that?'

'A certain circuit of cinemas is pledged to show it

whether it's their cup of tea or not. That means that a certain section of the public will go and see it whether it's the critics' cup of tea or not.'

'Do *you* think it's the critics' cup of tea?'

'I'm not sure,' said Mercedes. 'Lars did, of course. He called it Art. I call it Sex. One way or the other it's bound to be someone's cup of tea, and I daresay they'll get their money's worth whichever they come for.' Mercedes moved a couple of box-files from a chair and invited Hazel to sit down. 'Mant's in the projection room with most of the unit seeing the rushes. Getting abreast of the situation, he calls it. I'm straightening all the papers and refiling them under a three-letter system. He only knows the alphabet as far as C. You might as well stay. He's got to come back here.'

On the table in front of Mercedes was a dictaphone and a machine for shaving the wax cylinders for re-use. Mercedes took the last of six used cylinders from a rack, placed it on the machine and rapidly turned the handle, peeling off curled and powdery shavings of wax. That done, she placed the cylinder ready in the rack to take the impression of Mantobar's dictation. As she leaned forward to brush up the powderings of wax, she gave a little sharp cry. 'I wish I hadn't done that now,' she said, her fingers suddenly frozen into stillness round the little pile of dust. 'These must be pretty nearly his last words.'

Hazel didn't smile. 'Was that the only record?' she asked.

'It was the last,' said Mercedes. 'I did it automatically like I've always done it before. It was his voice talking, just giving me instructions, you know, and letters to type. And now it's gone.'

'They don't sound awfully like people's voices on a dictaphone, though, do they?' asked Hazel.

'It did to me,' replied Mercedes.

Hazel began to worry what Mercedes would do with the handful of wax dust, but didn't feel it was for her to suggest that she put it in an office envelope when clearly an urn must be what Mercedes had in mind. She looked around for a silver cigarette box or an alabaster ash-tray, but the lids of tin typewriter-ribbon boxes were the only visible ash-trays and they much too full of ash and stubs to suggest a desirable resting-place for Lars' last words. She raised her eyes to the dictaphone itself.

'The cylinder that's on the dictaphone has been partly used,' she said.

'Good heavens, so it has,' said Mercedes. 'I'd no idea.'

Depositing the dust on to a clean sheet of Pegasus-headed paper, she shifted the needle to the play-back position, lifted the mouthpiece and pressed the release. Squeaky and quite unrecognizable to anyone but Mercedes, Lars Porsen's voice came through.

'Friday afternoon; Memo after seeing rushes; do something about Coram's hair; still looks like a home perm. Do him good to be told, getting swelled head. . . . Mercy—check up on Paul's contract. Holly says Anglia-Rokewood wants him for a picture to start on the 27th of next month. Is his contract with us finished by then— he ought to be on call for if we need him after that. Is he? . . . Mercy, remind me to ask Mant why he hasn't sent us a publicity man. He's missing all the best stuff. . . .'

The rest of the cylinder was blank. Mercedes switched off and jotted briskly in her notebook. All sentiment forgotten, obeying 'Her Master's Voice.' Then she dialled Trunks and got through to the London office of Pegasus Pictures. While someone at the other end rustled through a contract file it occurred to Hazel that Lars had got his publicity man after all. Then Mercedes said, 'Oh, then we've got him till the twenty-fourth, and after that on call for another three weeks if required? Thanks,' and rang off.

Mercedes made another couple of notes and sat back a moment sunk in thought. Then she put a call through to Anglia-Rokewood's offices. She asked for Horace Float, with whom she appeared to be on fairly confidential terms. After a brief exchange of greetings she lowered her voice, 'Horace, there's talk that your boss wants our art man, Paul Heritage, on your next picture. How far's it gone, do you know? . . . oh . . . you wired him an offer on Friday evening? Paul can't have answered yet. . . . He *has?* Accepted. . . . But he couldn't. He's on call to us for three weeks after the date. . . . He said he'd *spoken* to Lars and Lars had agreed?—he *couldn't* have. Just a moment, when was Heritage's telegram handed in? Six twenty-five on Saturday at Steeple Tottering. I see . . .' Mercedes jotted wildly in her notebook. 'Well, thanks very much, Horace, I'll ring off now.'

Mercedes added a few more notes and then looked at

Hazel. 'You were in the "George" when a telegram came for Paul last Saturday, just after Lars had left for the Toad. Do you remember what Paul said?'

Unaware of her inference but conscious of Mercedes' tension, Hazel didn't speak.

'I do,' said Mercedes. 'He said that it hadn't taken a minute longer than twenty-four hours to be delivered. . . .' Her voice quickened. 'Anglia-Rokewood sent Paul a wire offering him a job on Friday evening. That wire reached Paul on Saturday evening at about five forty-five, after Lars had left. Paul couldn't accept that job without talking to Lars. He was under contract to us. But Paul did send a wire saying Lars had authorized him to accept—that evening at six twenty-five.' She had swung round from the table and was gripping Hazel's wrists by now. 'Do you realize what that means?'

'No,' said Hazel in a voice that creaked. 'No, I don't think so.'

'Paul must have seen Lars after he left the "George" on the night he died. He must have followed him up to the Toad. He was the last one to see him alive—and probably,' she lowered her voice and spoke slowly, 'the first one to see him dead.'

'You mean,' Hazel's voice sounded unreliable in her own ears, 'that Paul must have seen the accident?'

'Accident my foot. Paul hated Lars.'

'But everyone knows it was an accident. Lars rocked on the Toad.'

'How do we know he ever set foot on the Toad? How do we know he wasn't pushed over the cliff so that it would look as though he'd slipped off the Toad—by someone who had already worked up Lars' interest in the Toad in front of a lot of witnesses in the "George," so that they'd believe what he wanted them to believe.'

'But why? Why ever should he? Why would he want to?'

'Because he'd been in love with Lars' wife since before they were married.'

'He can't have been. He'd never met her.'

'That was the easiest way to be in love with Lars' wife, believe me. He wrote her letters. Don't worry, I saw them. I'm not making it up.'

'Did she show them to you?'

'She didn't have to. When Lars was in town I've often had to be secretary to both of them. Paul was in love with her all right, even if he didn't ever meet her. And he hated Lars although Lars was much too big-hearted even to realize. That's what happened. He got Lars talking about the Toad in public so that people would believe he'd rocked on the thing and fallen off, and then he killed him.'

'And *then* came down and sent a telegram proving he'd been the last person to see him alive?'

'Every murderer makes some mistake. Talking to Lars about the contract would be his excuse to catch him up near the Rock. If he'd just jumped out on him Lars would have been on guard, and he's a powerful man. No, Paul got talking, pushed him over, and then, with his mind in a turmoil, made his one false step of answering that telegram. And thank God he did or we would never have known.'

'But we don't know. There's no way in the world of proving that Lars didn't rock on the Toad.'

'Isn't there?' said Mercedes, her eyes narrow and sharp as a ferret's. 'Isn't there? There must be. There's going to be, and—my God, I think there is! Your lipstick!'

Hazel drew in a breath.

'You said it got lost on Friday evening. You said it rolled under the Toad. How many people rock on that Toad in any average week nowadays? No one. No one goes near it, do they?'

'No, no one remembers about it any more.'

'And after the accident the police put a barbed-wire fence round it, so no one could get near since. If the Toad had been rocked by Lars or anyone else, since you lost it on Friday evening, that lipstick will be squashed to pulp. That doesn't prove anything because someone else *might* have rocked it . . . but if the lipstick *isn't* squashed, then we can be absolutely certain that, however he met his death, Lars didn't rock on the Toad.'

Hazel felt like a small animal frozen to absolute stillness under the eye of a hovering hawk, in terror lest some flicker of fur or muscle should betray its presence at all. That was it, of course. That was the thing she should have remembered, the thing she had half-realized in her dream and that had totally vanished from her waking mind. Somehow or other, before Mercedes could do anything about it she had got to get that lipstick.

She said, 'I think you're absolutely brilliant. Will you tell the police?'

'The police? I don't know. You see I got a bit agitated when I was with them before and said I thought it was as good as murder, the way Paul had goaded him. They got rather impatient with me and called me an hysterical young woman. But if I went to them and *proved* that the Toad hadn't been rocked, they'd have to do something . . . what's the matter?'

Hazel had made an abrupt gesture of silence. She got to her feet. 'Someone listening,' she whispered and moved stealthily to the door. At the door she stood for a moment, while her body hid the lock, withdrawing the key. Stealthily she opened the door, stepped outside and equally stealthily closed it. She inserted the key, twisted it and put it in her pocket. Then she ran for dear life.

9

*I am happiest when I am idle. I could live for
months without performing any kind of labour, and at
the expiration of that time I should feel fresh and
vigorous enough to go right on in the same way for
numerous more months.*

ARTEMUS WARD

MANDRAKE had been having a lovely morning.
London, he decided, was at its best on a glorious
summer day when you had come up from the
country, had completed your business, and were due to
return before nightfall. Its merchandise, by comparison
with that available in a rural district, became rich and
desirable. Every moment had to be laid out to the best
possible advantage, and nothing, not even the chance
encounter with someone who bored you, could be
unduly prolonged. His talk for the B.B.C. 'Survey of
Origins' had been recorded and the rest of the day
was his own.

Already he had bought a specially designed razor
blade holder which made it theoretically impossible to
cut yourself while sharpening a pencil, three costly
sable paint-brushes, each finer and silkier than the last,
and half a dozen pencils in assorted B grades. Steeple

Tottering could offer him nothing between HB and 6B. 6B was much too coarse for Mandrake's taste, and while HB, properly sharpened, produced a line of admirable delicacy, it yielded but poorly to rubbing out. Mandrake did a lot of rubbing out.

He lunched at his club, and it now occurred to him that it might be an act of friendship to call on Angela Wingless, whom he had met on one or two occasions, and tell her anything she might wish to know about her husband's tragic end. He therefore put through a telephone call and presently took a taxi to her flat where he was shown into a sitting-room with green brocade curtains drawn against the sun.

In the sickly half-light Miss Wingless welcomed him and offered him tea and cigarettes. They sat on Petit Point and drank from Sèvres.

'I think you've never been here, have you, Professor?' she said. 'This is my own room. The rest of the house is Lars'.'

'It's an exquisite room,' said Mandrake. 'Apart from this I've only seen the hall. It certainly struck me as very rich.'

'Richness, that was it, of course. Everything about him was rich. That was the *thing* about Lars—his zest for living.' And the essential difference between them having thus been delicately established, Angela leaned forward and met his gaze with her enormous eyes. 'And now I am told he's dead—as though it is something possible to comprehend that Lars should be dead. Tell me—you tell me and try to make me believe it.'

So Mandrake did his best and Angela listened in total

silence and immobility. At the last he said, 'And now the unit is determined to prevent such a tragedy ever happening there again. They have decided that this rock is a danger to all reckless youths and they have arranged for a charge of dynamite to blast it off into the valley. I hope it won't pain you to learn that somehow the information has leaked out to certain Cinema News-reel companies and, I believe, the Television authorities, and that they have decided the ceremony should be recorded. It would appear that the aspect of the naked rock against the naked sky and then the slender figure of Elizabeth firing the charge and the thunderous explosion—all of it a sort of last memorial to your husband—is considered too moving for the public to be deprived of .'

Miss Wingless's blue-veined fingers replaced her cup in its saucer. 'Elizabeth?' she said.

'Elizabeth Brentbridge,' explained Mandrake. 'The actress who played the leading part in the film.' He rose. 'It is so charming of you to have received me. I felt that you ought to know all I was able to tell you—and about the ceremony—I feared it might be rather a shock if you came upon it for the first time in cold print. The occasion can hardly escape its portion of publicity.'

He pressed her fingers, picked up his parcels, crossed the Aubusson carpet and put his hand on the doorknob.

'Just a moment,' said Angela Wingless.

Hazel got a lift up the hill in a lorry taking chicken wire to Pennyfold. Her first intention was to retrieve the lipstick and, if it had not been crushed, get rid of it. Then she decided it would be quicker and simpler to ride the Toad herself and thus make sure it was crushed, and be gone before Mercedes arrived. She asked to be put down just before the bend in the road that led to her objective and did her best to saunter until the lorry was out of sight. As she came over the brow of the hill her heart sank. Not only was the Toad competently fenced in on its three exposed sides by barbed wire, but there was a small van parked near it with two men sitting on the step eating sandwiches.

She dodged hastily back out of sight and went a little way down the hill. It was hopeless to try and ride the Rock, but she might yet retrieve the lipstick. She broke off a long, pliable twig and went through the hedge to the left and then down through gorse and bramble till she was on the lower level that led to the stretch below the Toad. She kept under the rising cliff so that the men above could not possibly see her.

The Toad loomed greenish grey against the drifting white on the blue of the summer sky. It looked a long way up but not nearly so far as it had looked *down* on the occasion when she had ridden it. The rise of the cliff was not hopelessly sheer as she had imagined; here and there her eye could pick out footholds, twists of root, tufts of grass, jutting or receding bits of rock. She pushed the hazel twig down inside her dress so that it could not get lost, committed her somewhat crooked cause into her Maker's care and began the ascent.

As she clung and edged and thrust upwards and

slipped and clung again, she felt glad she had never subscribed to a fashion for long fingernails or been able to afford to smoke enough to destroy her wind. She was grateful, too, that her weight which so often she seemed to be supporting by one hand, was not considerable.

She had no way of knowing how long it would be before Mercedes arrived. She couldn't hope that locking the door would have seriously delayed her and Mercedes would probably take one of the studio cars. Manfred Mantobar might just have returned to his office in time to delay her but, in view of what Mercedes had said of his personality, Hazel couldn't feel that he would have succeeded for long.

Hazel's head was level with the turf, where, instead of overhanging as did the major part of the cliff-top, it dipped inwards a little, having been worn away under the Toad. She got her arms and chest over the top and managed to get enough grip on the turf to drag her legs and the rest of her body over the edge. She crouched there panting for a moment, then, making sure that she was hidden from the men by the Rock's bulk, worked the hazel twig out of her dress where it had become almost embedded in her flesh, poked it under the Rock and scraped.

She brought out a good deal of earthy dust, some blown dead leaves and a disgruntled colony of woodlice and then the twig broke two-thirds of the way up. Hazel went through her jacket pockets and found an emery board and two paper clips, made a splint for the twig and tried again, this time successfully. The lipstick rolled out, round and shiny and hideous as on the first day.

With a heart wildly pounding she put it in her pocket along with the twig and its embellishment and, not daring to look or think further than her first foothold, lowered herself gingerly over the edge of the cliff.

It seemed further going down but now there was triumph in her heart. Whether Mercedes could get anyone to listen or not, she couldn't prove without producing the lipstick that Lars *didn't* fall off the Toad unless she could persuade the police to lever off the Rock with crowbars and pulleys; and it was hard to imagine anyone going to quite that length for someone they regarded as an hysterical woman. Once Hazel's foothold slipped and, even while her fingers wound into a grass root, headlines flashed through her mind, 'Toad Claims Second Victim. Grim Find at Steeple Tottering.' But the grass root held and the headlines remained only a figment of the mind.

When she reached level ground she stood quite still while she felt in her pocket to be certain she hadn't lost the lipstick on the way down. It was there, safe, and as it lay in her curled fingers she heard Mercedes' voice, close behind her, saying, 'Give that to me.'

Hazel had not gone to all that trouble and risk to be tripped up by her gentle upbringing within sight of the goal. She doubled up, butted Mercedes in the middle and ran like a woman in a nightmare away from the Toad over the low open ground till she reached the gorse and bramble and plunged in.

Her upbringing, however, had been too gentle for her to butt hard enough, and Mercedes, unbalanced but not winded, was almost on her heels. They went twisting and stumbling through the prickly thickets and over the uneven, treacherous ground. Hazel would have kept to open country if she had not been out of breath after the climb. As it was, her only hope was to lose Mercedes for a moment in the undergrowth and be out of sight beyond the hedge before her pursuer could get clear. But Mercedes was as determined as she, and had the advantage of wearing slacks which made her practically indifferent to the prickles which slashed and tore at Hazel's legs. At the last, just as Hazel was beginning to gain, she was thrown by a loop of bramble which wrapped itself round her ankle. Half winded, she scrambled into a sitting position, snatched the lipstick from her pocket and threw it with all her strength into the densest thicket she could see just as Mercedes was on her.

'What was it?' gasped Mercedes. 'What did you throw?'

Hazel was past speaking for the present. Mercedes seized her by the shoulders. 'It was your lipstick, wasn't it, from under the Toad? I saw it flash.'

'No,' said Hazel, mustering a little breath. 'It was a diamond tiara.'

'Of course it was the lipstick. Was it crushed?' She began to shake Hazel, who made no attempt to answer, then suddenly she let go of her and plunged into the gorse in the direction of the thicket where the lipstick had vanished. Hazel stood up and, ripping her foot free of the bramble, headed for the clear ground, through the hedge and on to the road.

There were more people on the road than Hazel had ever seen there, a steady stream of townsfolk sprinkled with odds and ends from the film unit, all plodding industriously uphill towards the Toad. She began to be aware of her dishevelled appearance and of the blood that dripped here and there from the scratches on her legs. As she came over the hill for the second time that evening, she saw that the barbed wire had been taken away and the van had been moved back from the Toad and joined by several others bearing the letters and symbols of newsgathering concerns, one of which was the Television Outside Broadcast Unit. Two or three cameras had been set up while their operators moved to and fro, testing, focussing and making adjustments. Circling them and the Toad, spectators crowded thickly into an untidy ring, urged back by a couple of men who packed the charge under the rock and laid an inflammable trail from the Toad to the edge of the green.

Hazel remembered what she had hitherto forgotten—that this was the evening planned for the dynamiting of the Toad—and that once that had been accomplished no one could possibly prove Lars hadn't rocked on it. She began to pick out members of the Pegasus unit, then she noticed the Pegasus 'still' cameraman and the photographer from her own paper. Wormwell and his daughter were there and the barmaid from the 'George' but she couldn't see Paul anywhere.

As the larger unit car nosed over the hill, Hazel felt Paul standing just behind her. She turned her head.

'We had to come,' Paul whispered. 'I was in the middle of some work but this was a command perform-ance to swell the crowd in case the town didn't turn out in sufficient numbers.' Then, with concern on his face, 'Whatever's been happening to you?'

'I fell among thieves,' said Hazel. 'Don't look now, but the party's beginning.'

Unobtrusively dressed and still feverishly rehearsing the lines of the 'simple, human speech' with which Rollo had provided her. Elizabeth Brentbridge stepped out of the unit car. Rollo, who had been stationed by the Rock, advanced to meet her, took the flaming torch from a unit property man, placed it in her right hand and led her to the Toad. There he placed her left hand on the Rock and stood out of the picture.

'Hold it,' said the Pegasus still man and took a flashlight picture.

The man who had already put the dynamite under the Rock advanced quickly and nervously and ex-plained that the idea was to apply the torch to the *other* end of the trail, but Rollo said the speech must first be spoken with the Toad as background—other-wise the Toad would scarcely put in an appearance at all. The man agreed, but only if the torch, which was giving off an unhealthy amount of sparks, did not figure in the picture. He then took the torch to the other end of the trail and Elizabeth went into her speech.

But the sound recording men were not happy. There was too much background noise. In particular there was the long low hoot of a Klaxon horn coming nearer and nearer up the hill, that never faltered till the car drew up on the green; a larger, blacker car than any that was there already, a car, moreover, draped and decked with enormous black satin ribbons.

A uniformed chauffeur sprang from the driving seat, dashed round and opened the door which disgorged the epitome of grief, Angela Wingless, white faced, slight, black-veiled from head to foot, frail and stricken—but absolutely determined not to yield one inch of her position as chief mourner in this perfectly built-up scene.

Her voice was low, but pitched to reach the furthest corner of even an outdoor theatre and totally to annihilate the pale utterance of any merely film-trained performer like Elizabeth Brentbridge.

'I had to come. I feel it to be the last tribute I could pay to my husband's memory.' A white hand fluttered to her bosom. 'Thank heavens I'm not too late.'

Somebody went to meet her. Cameramen suspended themselves in mid-action. Elizabeth stopped her speech and looked like a nice little girl from a finishing school. Angela's gaze rested on her. 'Oh . . . yes . . . that little person in the jumper dress is Elizabeth Brentbridge, of course. So lovely of her to come too . . .'

Deftly she abstracted the torch from the hand that held it, then stood for a moment, bowed, with her fingers pressed to her temples, a monument of sorrow. Still cameras clicked. Somebody protested, 'Won't it upset you, Miss Wingless?'

She took her cue. 'No. Grief can never be assuaged, only sublimated in action. So I resolved to translate my sorrow into action on the behalf of others—to make the world free of this dangerous thing,' her gesture embraced the Rock 'that has already taken such cruel toll. That is my tribute to the man whose love has been my support and stay these four or five years . . . so ardent . . . such a boy at heart. And to think,' the superb voice broke, 'that it was that very boyishness which was so lovable that has been his undoing.' A tremulous smile flashed and faded. 'And yet I would not have changed him. In death as in life he was inevitably, triumphantly himself. It was to be. It could not have been otherwise, and I for one must say that he died, as he had lived, accepting life's challenge to the hilt, and it is probably the way he would have chosen. . . . Do I light this little fuse here?'

'*Miss Wingless, Miss Wingless.*' It was Mercedes' hoarse and breathless whisper at her elbow. 'Stop. Don't touch the fuse. Lars was murdered. It will destroy the evidence. . . .'

Angela turned the look of uncomprehending annihilation on the interruption that she would have turned on a dropped tea-tray in the stalls. 'Don't be silly, dear. We're on the air,' she whispered, and touched the torch to the trail.

Graceful as ever but with admirable swiftness, she moved back to the first line of spectators, to watch the flame lick backwards to the Toad, till with a fizzle and splutter and final roar the earth opened below the Rock, which, propelled at last from its balance, heaved over and went thundering into the valley.

'And that,' said a voice close to Hazel's ear, 'could be justly described as another Wingless Victory.'

Hazel spun round and regarded Paul's profile a moment.

'Yes,' she agreed unhappily and, for once, not even sincerely. 'She is wonderful, isn't she.'

But whatever Paul might have replied she never heard, for Mercedes had gone into hysterics. It seemed only fitting that someone should and Angela was clearly not the hysterical type while Elizabeth, totally eclipsed, had almost ceased to be a type at all.

Angela was now most considerately asking if the press had all the photographs it required, and even gathering Elizabeth and Mercedes into the picture, casting an arm round each and drawing them both to her bosom so that they perforce had their backs or at best their profiles to the camera while she brooded above with the compassionate full-face of a more deeply-felt and infinitely nobler grief.

Paul's hand fell on Hazel's arm. 'Let's get away before they commit suttee,' he said quietly.

'What is suttee?'

'Don't you know? Where *were* you educated?'

'In Steeple Tottering.'

'Yes, of course. The wives of Indian rulers used to burn themselves on their husband's funeral pyre. I believe it was rather well thought of.'

Suddenly she thought, 'That's what it is. He's jealous that she should have spoken of her husband as though she were fond of him. All he'd been thinking of was that now, at last, she would be free, and she is only thinking of her husband.'

'But he'll have to speak to her,' she thought compassionately. 'I must make it easy for him. If things go wrong—if Mercedes manages to convince someone— he might never see her again after all he's done for her.'

Aloud she said, 'Please don't take me away yet. I want to look at Angela Wingless.'

'Do you?'

'Yes, of course. So do you.'

Paul didn't answer. They stood in silence on the fringe of the crowd. Hazel began to move nearer the road so that Angela would have to pass them on the way to her car. Mercedes was still gasping in urgent incoherence to Angela who suddenly gave a little cry of exasperation and slapped her sharply on both cheeks. Mercedes stopped in mid cry, almost spat at Angela, then gathered herself and began to run across the grass, past Hazel, through the crowd and on down the hill. Her face was working and, as she passed, Hazel heard the words, gasped through shut teeth, 'The police. I'll go straight to the police.'

Rollo had joined the group round Angela. It was not admittedly the performance, nor indeed the performer that he had rehearsed, but it had been magnificent in its way and would ensure the right type of publicity for Pegasus Pictures. He was delighted with Angela and was introducing her to those members of the unit whom she had not met, as she made a leisured and triumphal détour towards the car. As they came within earshot, Hazel heard her saying to Gussie, 'Oh yes, my husband told me you were brilliant with the camera—and—oh, isn't there an art man he used to talk about, who'd been an architect?'

Elaborately casual as the words were meant to appear, Hazel suddenly knew it was important to Angela to meet Paul.

'That would be Paul,' said Gussie. 'He must be somewhere about.'

'It's all right,' Hazel told herself. 'I'm glad. It would have been dreadful if she'd ignored him.' And her heart sank lower and lower.

' "And when Thyself with shining foot shall pass," ' Paul quoted in a scarcely audible whisper.

Hazel started to step backwards, meaning to disappear, but his hand on her arm tightened its grip. So Paul must have need of her to bolster up his *amour propre;* to suggest perhaps that he was not totally dependent on Angela's interest; that he had a separate existence. She stood, frozen into a 'property' woman while Gussie introduced them.

Hazel watched the slender fingers flutter into Paul's and stay there a trifle longer than they need have, saw the enormous, violet-shadowed eyes widen and deepen as they gazed into Paul's before the lashes trembled downwards, heard the faint intake of breath before she spoke, and felt the impact of it all on Paul as though it had been on herself.

'Paul—Paul Heritage. The name seems so oddly

familiar. Of course, Lars told me such a lot about you all.'

'It would sound foolish if I were to say that the words Angela Wingless convey a great deal to me?'

'Foolish? I don't know. Foolish things are very—delightful sometimes.'

'This is Hazel Fairweather,' said Paul, relinquishing Hazel's wrist. 'She admires you very much.'

'So sweet of you.' Angela's eyes widened and deepened again as she gazed into Hazel's. 'Another of the unit?'

'Nobody at all really. I just live here and work in an office,' said Hazel, wildly effacing herself from this conversation into which she felt she had no right to have entered. Angela pressed her fingers and returned her eyes to Paul's.

'I'm putting up at the "George" just for the night,' she said.

'At the "George"? There isn't any room, is there?' Paul had said, before he and Hazel and everyone remembered that Lars wasn't using his room any more.

'Oh, yes,' said Angela, 'we telephoned and they said they'd manage something just for the night. There's room for one more in the car. Shall I run you down?'

As soon as he had relinquished her wrist Hazel had been edging out of the group and now she took a firmer step backwards and began to walk briskly away. She had done her part and nothing more could surely be required of her. 'Herself with shining foot' had not only remembered him, but was clearly as delighted to meet him in the flesh as he could possibly have hoped. Whatever was to come, Paul was unquestionably going to be vouchsafed his hour. As she went past Angela's car she saw a face at the window and realized that the back seat was occupied by Mandrake. She began to walk faster and faster, passing groups of townspeople on their way home, and, as it was beginning to be dusk, it scarcely mattered that tears were running down her scratched and grubby face. It was quite five minutes before Paul caught up with her.

10

My golden hair was getting loose
Yet fell I out on that excuse?
Not so:

OWEN SEAMAN

'WHY did you run away?' said Paul.

'I didn't,' said Hazel. 'I went.'

'She ended up by offering you a lift too, when she found she couldn't separate me from you. And then you'd vanished. They're going to drive down very slowly and stop to pick us up when they see us in the headlights.'

'I *can't* be picked up by a car,' said Hazel wildly. 'Have a bit of sense and look at me.'

Paul looked.

'You're scratched and bloody and torn and dirty and, good heavens, I believe you're crying. Look, let's get through the hedge and wait till the car's gone past. Is that a good idea?'

It was a splendid idea. When they were through the hedge Hazel said, 'But you may never see her again,' and Paul replied, 'Now start at the beginning and tell me what's been happening to you.'

'Did you only leave her so that you could find out if I was in trouble?'

'No. Are you?'

'No.'

'I left her because I felt that it was the right thing to do. Anything after her big scene would have been such an anti-climax.'

'Her scene?'

'The sorrowing widow. It was superb—her clothes, her timing. If she'd arrived a fraction sooner it would have been too soon for the fullest effect; a fraction later and it would have been merely anti-climax. Angela Wingless is an artist.'

'She was glad to see *you*.'

'Oh, yes. No one's questioning her versatility.'

Wheels could be heard scrunching over the rough gravel. Screened by the hedge Paul turned his head to watch the big car go slowly down the road. On his face was a smile that faintly mocked himself. Under his breath he began to quote:

' "Look thy last on all things lovely
    Every hour . . .
    Since all things that thou would'st praise,
    Beauty took from those who loved them
    In other days."

'Only,' he went on, 'de la Mare was talking nonsense when he said "beauty." He should have said, "reality." Isn't it odd? I'd have gone to the gallows for her sincerity.'

Hazel said, 'I know.' Then rather awkwardly she

added, 'But it wouldn't be reasonable to go now, so please don't be careless.'

'To go where?'

'To the gallows.' Hazel felt agonizingly embarrassed, but she knew she couldn't let him go down to the town without telling him what was waiting for him. She said, 'You thought—I thought it too—that she was the sort of woman a man might have to die for—but if she isn't'—the words came out in a rush now—'you don't have to die, anyway, just out of carelessness.'

'I never thought of dying.'

'Then please be careful because Mercedes thinks . . .'

'Mercedes? For the love of goodness where does Mercedes come into it?'

'She thinks you murdered Lars.' It was said. Hazel turned her face away and felt it slowly growing crimson. . . .

'In the name of wonder, why?' asked Paul, blank amazement on his face.

'Somebody murdered him.'

'How do you know?'

'Lars never rocked on the Toad at all. Nobody could have rocked on it after my lipstick rolled under it the day before. I got my lipstick out, uncrushed, just before they arrived to dynamite the rock—and Mercedes knows it.'

'And where do I come in?'

'Anglia-Rokewood Films had a telegram from you; the time of dispatch proved that you were probably the last person to see him alive.'

'Good heavens, I suppose it did.'

'And Mercedes knows that—and you were in love with Angela.'

'Did Mercedes know *that*?'

'Yes. She used to read Angela's letters.'

'I see. The whole thing looks pretty tidy, doesn't it?'

'It's tidier than that. Mandrake found a pile of freshly-pulled yarrow and a packet of book-matches with my name pencilled on it near the Toad, just after he found the body.'

'Your name?'

'Yes. I'd written it on the packet I lent you a few moments before you left the "George." '

'Does Mandrake know you'd lent it to me?'

'No.'

'What does he think?'

'Well, up to a point he thinks that I was *in flagrante* with Lars, and that the whole thing was so exhilarating that Lars rocked on the Toad and fell off and I dropped my matches. . . .'

'He can't believe that; no one could.'

'He knew that's what I should have said if he'd mentioned those points at the inquest.'

'Good Lord!' Paul lifted her abruptly to her feet and began to wriggle through the hedge.

'Where are we going?'

'Down to the police station, of course.'

'Wouldn't it be even better to go in the opposite direction?'

'Not on your life.' He was walking fast and Hazel had to run to keep up with him. 'Look here, child, there's one question I don't have to ask. You think I killed him, don't you? It's all right, you don't have to answer.' He turned in his stride and looked at her but kept on walking. 'I'm not even sure I can prove it, but between you and me and God, my dear, I didn't kill him, for whatever comfort it may be to you. You don't have to try and believe it.'

'Of course I believe it.'

Hazel's heart began to sing. She had been prepared to love him and succour him, on the run, with blood on his hands and another woman in his heart, but now everything was perfect. She broke into a trot at his side. 'Do you *have* to go to the police?' she asked. 'I know wonderful places to hide.'

Paul stood still in the middle of the road and regarded her. On his face was a mixture of amazement and disbelief. 'You make me feel so very, very old,' he said, and began to walk again.

'That means you think I'm a perfect fool.'

'You show a marked determination to preserve me alive at any cost, and that may be foolish, but it has its endearing side. Only, don't you see, if Mercedes has gone to the police with her information, my disappearance at this stage would be the very worst thing that could happen?'

'Not the worst thing. The worst thing that could happen would be—would be——' Hazel couldn't say it.

'Ah, yes, the gallows.' He completed it for her. 'That would be very nasty indeed. You see, I did take the car and follow Lars to the Toad after I got that telegram. Actually he was rather decent about letting me accept the offer, which irritated me in a way, because I disliked him so much. Then I left him and sent my answering telegram and went back to the "George." There didn't seem any particular point in mentioning it to anyone. It didn't add to or subtract from any of the facts, but I see now it would have been more sensible to tell them than to let them find out. Now, I suppose, my part looks more sinister every minute.'

Hazel began to notice a glow in the sky, but as they rounded the next bend a vast dark shadow lumbered into view, coming up the hill from the town, and took her mind off everything else.

'Hullo,' a voice came booming at them. 'Is that you, Hazel? Are you all right?'

'Yes, thank you, Professor,' called Hazel. 'And you?'

'Don't be silly.' The professor came panting towards them. 'We crawled in that car all the way to the town, looking for you. As there wasn't a sign of you I began to worry, so I came back.'

'That doesn't sound like you, Professor,' said Paul. 'Are you sure it wasn't me you were worrying about?'

'Shall we go on now?' asked Mandrake, ignoring Paul's question. 'There won't be anything left fit to eat.'

Hazel said quietly, 'It's all right, you know. Paul knows what you think and what I thought. He was with Lars at the Toad a little while before he died, but he didn't kill him.'

'Did he say so?'

'Yes.'

'Then, of course, that makes everything all right.'

'Don't be silly,' said Hazel. 'He's going to the police now, of his own accord, to tell them all about it.'

'Can he prove it?'

'No. And I've offered to "hide him in the foothills," and he won't hear of it. If he'd been guilty he'd have jumped at it, wouldn't he?'

'Would he?' Mandrake pondered, then to Paul he said, thoughtfully, 'Would you?'

Paul said, 'I haven't an idea *how* I should behave if I were guilty.'

'That was neat,' admitted Mandrake. 'Have you any objection to telling us what did take place between you and Porsen on that occasion?'

'I followed him up to the Toad.'

'How did you know you'd find him there?'

'He used to disappear every evening at the same time. The previous evening Hazel and I had been sitting by the Toad and he didn't see us but spread himself out and took a nap. We assumed it to be a regular occurrence.'

'Did anyone else know where he went?'

'Not to my knowledge. He always drove the car up the hill after the day's shooting and was back at the "George" in time for dinner.'

'I see. And you came upon him, at what time?'

'About twenty-five past five. I took the car up in a tearing hurry, hoping to catch him before he went to sleep. I wanted to ask him a favour and I didn't think I stood much chance of success if I had to wake him up to ask it.'

'Did you have to wake him?'

'No. He was sitting on the grass and he didn't even seem annoyed to see me. I showed him the offer I'd had in the telegram and he seemed rather pleased. It appeared he'd heard a rumour that this other firm wanted me, and he'd imagined I'd been trying to negotiate something behind his back, whereas actually the wire was the first I'd heard of it. Lars likes to be in on things.'

'You were sitting with him on the grass then, for about how long?'

'Not more than ten minutes. I suppose I must have pulled out the yarrow automatically while we were talking. And I must have dropped Hazel's book-matches.'

'Did you happen to notice me sketching below in the valley? I must have been there at the time.'

'No. We were too far away from the edge to see anyone in the valley or for anyone to have seen us.'

'Then he was too far to have rolled over by accident in his sleep,' said Mandrake. 'And when you left him, at about twenty-five to six, what was he doing?'

'I looked round as I got into the car. He was just spreading his silk handkerchief on the grass under his head prior to going to sleep.'

'No one else was in sight?'

'No.'

'And you didn't think to mention it to the police?'

'No.'

'And now you think you will?'

'Mercedes can prove I was the last known person to see him alive and is convinced I killed him. I'd sooner go to them before they start looking for me.'

'They're looking for you already,' said Mandrake. 'They were inquiring for you before I left.'

'So Mercedes convinced them,' said Hazel.

'Possibly; but there's something else.'

Mandrake was watching Paul narrowly. As they rounded the last bend in the lane they could see what had caused the glow in the sky; a little beyond the town to the right, in what had been the aerodrome, was a towering inferno of flames. The hangar was ablaze.

'The studio,' said Paul. 'The studio's on fire.'

'It is thought it must have started a matter of moments after the unit left for the dynamiting ceremony, for it to have got such a hold,' said Mandrake. 'Even the nightwatchman was at the Toad. It was the first time the studio had been entirely empty since the Pegasus unit took possession——'

'Empty?' ejaculated Paul. 'I left my tools out——'

Mandrake plodded on regardless of the interruption, 'The fireman's theory is that it must have started somewhere in the artist's workshop.'

But Paul had begun to run in the direction of the hangar. Mandrake and Hazel also hurried, but Paul's long legs quickly outstripped them. As he turned out of the lane and along the right-hand fork of the one brightly-lit main road they saw the local policeman waylay him, and after a few moments rather agitated conversation they watched Paul and the policeman make their way along the other arm of the road, towards the police station.

'It's a pity he had to be running the wrong way,' said Mandrake. 'Giving himself up might have been quite a point in his favour.'

'He forgot about everything except the fire,' said Hazel. 'He'd been dragged off to the Toad in the middle of doing some work. It was only natural he should try and save his tools. You should have told him the place was on fire when you met us.'

'I wanted to watch his face when first he saw it,' explained Mandrake. 'The fire wasn't an accident. It was deliberately started. A petrol can was missing from one of the unit cars, and it was found empty, behind the hangar.'

'So that's why you pretended to have come looking for me,' said Hazel furiously. 'You wanted to catch him out. You think he murdered Lars *and* set fire to the hangar, don't you?'

Mandrake continued to walk in silence for a little while. 'Actually,' he said at last, 'I don't think your young man can have had anything to do with either catastrophe.'

'You don't? Why not?'

'Chiefly because he is, so patently, your young man and not Angela Wingless'. The only possible motive he could have had was his being in love with the man's wife. But after careful consideration I couldn't feel that anyone would go to quite that length unless he'd positively had some human contact with the lady. Thinking it over last night I realized that I couldn't be sure that he hadn't, but it seemed that if we got them together we could easily tell. So I dropped in at her Knightsbridge flat this afternoon.'

'You went up to London for that?'

'No, not for that. The local shop had run out of one-B pencils, so I had to go up. I looked her up in passing. When I mentioned the scheme for dynamiting the rock and the publicity it was likely to entail she began to feel that it was her place, as chief mourner, to be here.'

'And you were satisfied with the result?'

'The slow boat to China proved to be even slower than I had anticipated. Young Heritage couldn't wait to get away from her and go in search of you. We must, of course, consider that this course might be a deliberate ruse to disarm suspicion, but if it was, you'd know. Was it?'

Hazel looked him squarely in the face. 'He isn't "my young man," if that's what you mean.'

'Is he hers?'

'I don't think so. Oh, I don't know, do I? He seemed awfully disappointed about her. She wasn't a bit what he'd expected.'

'Then he can't have met her before, in which case I, personally, think it very unlikely that he killed her husband.'

'It's going to be awfully subtle, though, isn't it, convincing the police of that after what Mercedes has told them?'

'What has Mercedes told them?'

'That he's been in love with Angela for years and

she's read his letters; that he hated Lars and was the last person to see him alive and that Lars never fell off the Toad.'

'How does she know?'

Hazel told him.

'So that would account for your general appearance of having just fought a protracted but losing battle with a porcupine. I didn't like to mention it before.'

'How very considerate of you,' said Hazel, who nevertheless found it impossible altogether to dislike Mandrake now that he seemed to consider that Paul might not be guilty.

They had reached the fire and stood, some way off, watching the final disintegration of the hangar, which was now no more than a red-hot, empty shell. Cameras, projectors, film and stock were all things of the past. Nothing remained of the entire enterprise but the human beings, all of whom had been at the Toad. Manfred Mantobar ran clucking in little circles, wringing his soft white hands.

'Everything gone,' he moaned. 'Every scrap of film and all the equipment. It always happens to me. It's a hoodoo. It's a jinx. There's always been a jinx on anything I undertake.'

Mandrake watched dispassionately. 'It would appear that someone hated Lars and all his works.'

'You think this was done by the same person?' said Hazel.

'Why not?'

'Then you must know it wasn't Paul. Paul hated

Lars but he was proud of the work he'd done on this picture. He wouldn't destroy it.'

'They think the fire was started in his workshop.'

'How can anyone tell where a fire started?' said Hazel. 'I think they just said that to give them an excuse to ask Paul some more questions after what Mercedes told them. What will they do to him?'

'Question him, I suppose, and make sure that he doesn't leave the district. They'd hardly lock him up, yet. The pity is that he can't prove he didn't do it.'

'No. We shall have to do that.'

'How?'

'By finding out who did. Or has the whole thing lost its charm for you now that the police have begun to take an interest?'

'Don't be unkind,' said Mandrake. 'If my mind seems to wander it's just that I'm frightfully hungry and I can't think how to get you safely home to your mother.'

'I've got a bicycle at the office.'

'You can't career about darkest Sallowshire at dead of night on a bicycle.'

'It isn't dead of night, and anyway I often do.'

'Well, that's all right so long as I don't know, but this evening I do,' explained Mandrake miserably. 'Besides, you're in a simply shocking state of disrepair. I ought to put you in a taxi but there isn't one. I'm at my wits' end.'

'Actually there's a single-decker bus every two hours,' Hazel reassured him. 'I've just missed one, but there's the last one at ten. I'll go by that if you'll feel better. I've got ages to catch it.'

Mandrake smiled. 'Then we'll go and find out if there's any dinner left at the "George." You must be ravenous too.'

Cheerfully he began to lead her towards the inn.

'But you can't be seen with me in the "George" in my state of disrepair, and I've just realized what I did with my bag. I left it in Mercedes' office at the hangar. I've neither comb nor lipstick nor powder.'

'Couldn't we borrow some from Angela or Elizabeth?'

'I'd rather ask the barmaid.'

'What a good idea. She's a most amiable young woman and much better made-up than either of them.'

So Mandrake handed her over to Connie who led her off for repairs while Mandrake went into the dining-room to speak for a couple of dinners.

'Did you get to see the fire as well, Miss?' asked the barmaid eagerly. 'I only got an hour to see the Toad blasted off, so I had to miss the fire. Proper blaze-up, wasn't it?'

Hazel assured her it had been splendid.

'S'pose all the film and that must have burnt to a cinder, won't it, or would there be a copy kept somewhere else?'

'I gather it's all burnt,' said Hazel. 'Mr. Mantobar was awfully upset.'

'After all the trouble they been to,' said Connie with pleasurable sorrow. 'All those London actresses and actors, and Mr. Wormwell's sheep having to be dyed and I dunno what all. Would you like the "Kissproof" or the "Florida Firefly"? I always carry two, then I can make a change when I want to cheer myself up. "Firefly's" ever such a red red.'

Hazel decided on the 'Kissproof.'

'It isn't really, though,' said Connie. 'Nothing is. I suppose they've got to call them something. Pity about Peggy Wormwell's part though. She had a part in the picture all to herself. Now we'll never see what she was like in it.'

'How did you know?'

'She said so.'

'When?'

'To-night, as we were coming down the hill.'

'Did she know the hangar was on fire?'

'Well, we saw it from the distance as we came down into the town.'

'Was it before or after you noticed the fire that she told you about her part?'

'I don't know. While we was watching it, I think. Or just before. I've never seen such a big fire. Of course she was able to go on and have a good look close to, but I had to come back into the "George." She said Mr. Porsen had told her she had quite a future in pictures. And now nobody'll ever know. Bit of hard luck, isn't it? Do you powder on top of your lipstick?' she broke off to exclaim. 'Takes off the gloss, I think.'

'I suppose it does,' said Hazel, 'but if I didn't I'd be afraid of making marks on things.'

'There's always that,' admitted Connie. 'But you got to look your best in work like mine. Funny how Miss

Brentbridge never seems to try. You'd think she would, in her job. I should.'

'Yes,' agreed Hazel. 'You'd think she would.'

'That Angela Wingless took the shine out of her, up at the Toad.' Connie's face glowed with happy malice. 'I'd never heard of her before, but it seems she's a theatre actress from London. Made Miss Brentbridge look like two pennorth of coppers. Now *she* behaved how you'd expect a leading lady to behave, didn't she?'

'She did, indeed. She's staying here the night, isn't she?'

'Yes. She's just finishing her dinner in the dining-room with that Miss Mercy.'

'Mercedes?' Hazel had no idea what her surname might be, nor it seemed had Connie. 'Has she come back?'

'Yes, she came in not so long ago and went over and sat at Miss Wingless' table. They're in there now.'

Hazel thanked Connie for her help, tipped her with the half-crown Mandrake had given her for the purpose and went into the dining-room. Mercedes passed her in the doorway looking a little like the cat that had eaten the canary. Hazel's eye ran round the room and she saw Mandrake first and then Angela, some distance apart, both alone at their tables. Determinedly she crossed the room in Angela's direction and came to a halt in front of her. Miss Wingless lifted her eyes in a gaze of complete non-recognition.

'Miss Wingless,' said Hazel, 'if you're not expecting anyone, please would you have coffee at our table? I'm with Professor Mandrake over there—and I've wanted to meet you all my life.'

Angela smiled faintly. 'But I've just had coffee,' she protested.

'Couldn't you have some more?'

'I suppose I could. All right. I'll join you in a moment.'

Hazel thanked her and went over to Mandrake and told him what she'd done. 'You see, we've got to find out what she'll say about Paul if the police decide to question her.'

'Do you think she'll tell us?'

'I don't know.'

The 'joint' course arrived, a largish flat area of fat surrounded by a sliver of grey lean and coated with gravy. There was a morsel of string, too, on Hazel's plate, which looked surprisingly appetizing.

As Hazel helped herself to vegetables a coolness and a flicker of draperies bore upon them. Mandrake rose and bowed Angela into a chair. He offered her a drink and she refused. Hazel said, 'I saw you in "The Blossoming Thorn" and "Summer Lightning," and "Illyria Revisited." I never thought you'd come to Steeple Tottering.'

For the next ten minutes Angela bathed in the warm golden glow of past successes; then, having emptied her plate, Hazel drew in a quick breath and took the plunge.

'Has Mercedes been to the police?' she said abruptly.

Miss Wingless looked hideously jolted. Her husband had not been a bad husband in his way, unfaithful certainly, and in a completely different class from hers as an artist, but never unkind or ungenerous. She had been quite tired of him for a long time, but such as he was, he was dead. She had played her part as his widow magnificently, small though it had been. Now like any other performer she was entitled to her due of praise, while all she had got so far was an anti-climactic outburst about murder from her husband's hysterical continuity-girl. The thing was done with. Nice little man that he had been, she had laid him to rest quite adequately. Now she wanted to relax. If it was going to start all over again it was really the end.

'She has been to the police,' said Angela, 'with a perfectly silly story about a young man pushing Lars over the cliff.'

'Of course you don't believe it?'

'I didn't really listen. I was all jangled and upset. I do think she might have tried to consider my feelings.'

'She's been bothering the police already,' said Hazel. 'I think she must have been a bit in love with your husband.'

'Oh, I've always known it. That type of woman is always in love with somebody's husband.'

'I think his dying so suddenly has unbalanced her a bit. She feels she's got to pin the blame on someone. I expect she'll try and drag you into it, too—try and get the police to interview you.'

'Yes, that's the tiresome thing. They'd never have bothered me if she hadn't bothered them. They sent word that someone would call on me in the morning for a few routine questions. And I wanted to make an early start. I'm rehearsing at ten-thirty.'

Hazel remembered her position as a Wingless fan. 'Oh, do tell me?' she said, leaning forward.

'Just a little thing for the Third Programme,' said Angela, feeling instantly better. 'A little bit of Proust.'

'Oh, what a shame,' said Hazel, 'to think that you're going to allow a mischievous hysterical woman to make so much trouble just to get her name in the papers.'

'I'm not *allowing* it,' protested Angela. 'I can't prevent it.'

'You could if you wanted to. After all, you're the one concerned. Do you think Mr. Heritage ought to be tried for murder?'

'Of course not.'

'Then if you simply put your foot down and say that Mr. Porsen always took a nap after dinner and occasionally walked in his sleep, she wouldn't have a leg to stand on. It would have been the easiest thing in the world for anyone sleep-walking to have gone over the cliff. The Toad being rocked or not rocked wouldn't affect it. The thing would remain the accident it so evidently was, you'd be at your rehearsal and Mercedes wouldn't be able to bring everything personal or delicate in your married life into the publicity of a trial.'

'I see,' said Angela. 'Yes, I do see. Lars did take a nap before dinner whenever he had the chance. Of course I never actually remember his walking in his sleep, but I couldn't swear he didn't. I'm sure most people do sometimes.'

'I don't,' said Mandrake. 'Do you?'

Hazel looked at him with dislike.

'No,' admitted Angela. 'I don't. Lars didn't either. It would be dangerous to say he did.'

'However could it be dangerous?' asked Hazel.

'Because if Mercedes did manage to get the thing as far as a trial, and if I had testified that Lars sometimes walked in his sleep, she would very certainly find people to testify that he didn't,' her lip curled downwards, 'even if she had to do it herself. It would be a little unwise for me to say anything that might prejudice a jury against me. It would be better to keep simply to the truth.'

'And the truth is?'

'Well, I'm bound to admit Paul did write me some rather foolish letters, though I wouldn't say I gave him a lot of encouragement. I certainly never imagined there'd be anything like—this.' Her eye grew remote. Hazel realized that she was suddenly seeing herself in a highly dramatic, public rôle in a *cause celèbre*, and not altogether disliking herself in the part. 'Of course,' already the voice embraced the possibility of a larger, tenser audience than just Mandrake and Hazel in the 'George,' 'one can never know . . . in one's ignorance, never foresee exactly to what lengths that poetic type will go when it falls deeply in love.'

Hazel began to see what she was up against.

11

The early bird got up and whet its beak;
The early worm arose, an easy prey.

OWEN SEAMAN

HAZEL spoke brutally into her reverie. 'Miss Wing-less, you can't honestly suppose that Paul killed your husband.'

Angela smiled ethereally. 'I'd be the last to suggest it. But if it *is* suggested and it all comes out in court about Paul's letters, it would be very unwise for me to be found out in some invention like Lars' sleep-walking. That would make it look as though I had some *interest* in clearing Paul. It might even look as though *I* had been in love with *him* and wanted Lars out of the way. I owe it to my husband's memory not to get involved in anything like that.'

'You must know Paul wouldn't do it.'

'I don't know Paul at all. I only met him this evening.'

'And from that meeting did you get the impression that he was a man who would kill for love of you?'

The moment she'd said it, Hazel realized that it was

a blow below the belt and wasn't going to do a bit of good. The shadowed lids veiled the enormous eyes and gave Hazel a moment in which to study her adversary. The hair, which was of no particular colour, waved back from a noble, flawless brow; the nose was delicately boned, and only the merest fraction longer than absolutely necessary, giving an air of infinite breeding and fragility; the eyes were greenish-grey and large and deeply set, but though they were not particularly dark, when open they blazed out on the world with something like hypnotic power. The upper lip was a trifle long, the mouth wide, the lips thin and almost cruel. The throat showed white between the dark chiffon folds of the scarves that were wound round it and secured by a large antique brooch.

It was a face that could never have been called pretty, though it could easily become lovely or terrible or divine, tragic or dissolute—or even—as it had on the last two occasions of its owner's West End appearance—exquisitely insane. At the moment, however, with eyes shadowed, it was without life or colour or any existence of its own, like an emptied vessel waiting to be filled with whatever emotion it should next be called upon to contain. But when the eyes opened the face had a 'fated' look, an air of dedication to a high, strange destiny. Hazel recognized that Angela had plumped flatfooted for the rôle of *femme fatale*.

'No,' at last replied Angela from several steps out of this world, 'he didn't give that impression to anyone else, did he? When we shook hands he tore his fingers from mine as though they'd been singed and only his eyes lingered on my face.' Her lips curved and her eyes dwelt with infinite compassion on their inward picture. 'And then he refused to ride with me and went away down the hill. I might have been hurt if I hadn't *known*, here,' the fingers fluttered to the heart, 'although then I didn't understand. . . .'

'What do you understand now?' Hazel asked almost angrily.

'He didn't want to involve *me* in anything, poor boy; poor foolish, impetuous boy.'

' "Thought and affliction, passion, hell itself,
    She turned to favour and to prettiness." '
muttered Hazel ill-advisedly.

'What, dear?' Angela leaned forward attentively. 'Oh yes, Ophelia. Only of course it was her father.' She considered the rôle and decided it had nothing to add to the one she had already chosen, before her feet brushed the earth again. 'I suppose I shall have to do something about this rehearsal. I'd probably better telephone someone.' She looked vaguely about as though a telephone might reasonably be expected to appear on the table.

'Can I do it for you?' offered Hazel with sudden misgiving. If Angela telephoned she would almost certainly do it from the public telephone in the bar and would have everybody spellbound with her performance of the *femme fatale*. Paul's pathetic romance would be public property in a matter of moments.

'You, dear?' said Angela. 'How sweet of you. No, I think I ought to see to it myself. There must be a telephone somewhere. . . .'

'There's one in a cubicle past the reception desk,' said Hazel, but Angela had already approached a waiter.

'I'm going to try and head her off,' whispered Hazel to Mandrake, 'or she'll tell everybody everything.'

Someone at the next table had risen too and pushed back a chair in Hazel's path so that she had to make a considerable detour. By the time she got into the bar Angela was in possession of the public telephone, and over her shoulder, coming wearily into the hotel, Hazel saw Paul. She flew to meet him.

'Come and have a drink,' she said. 'You look as though you need one.'

'What I need,' replied Paul, 'is a couple of steaks.'

'Well, *I* need support,' persisted Hazel, her fingers once more taking their grip on his wrist. 'Please stand exactly where I put you.'

Determinedly she led him into the bar and manœuvred him into a position in which Angela couldn't fail to meet his eye the moment she looked up. Angela was speaking into the receiver in a voice which, though technically a whisper, was so charged with secret urgency that it commanded instant silence in every corner of the bar.

'Bernard,' she was saying, 'is that you? Yes, it's Angela Wingless. . . . Look, my dear, I'm afraid I'll have to ask you to ring the B.B.C. first thing in the morning and tell them I may not be able to get to the rehearsal . . . yes . . . well you knew I motored down this evening about poor Lars' sudden death . . . yes,' she lowered her voice to an even more penetrating whisper, 'well, things have turned out a little more complicated . . . I can't mention names, but . . .'

Hazel rapped sharply on the counter and said, loudly, 'What are you drinking, Mr. Heritage?'

Angela lifted her eyes and saw Paul and for a moment something like embarrassment showed on her face.

'No,' she spoke again into the receiver. 'I can't go into it now. It's just something I hadn't anticipated. Of course I shall be there if I possibly can, but do ring them, won't you? I'm going to lie down, now. It *has* all been a little upsetting.'

She replaced the receiver, smiled remotely and wafted up the stairs to her room. Connie picked up the receiver. 'How much was that London call, please?' she asked and made a note on a captive pad. She then looked at Paul and said, 'Yes, sir?'

'It's all right now,' said Hazel, and smiled at Connie. 'We don't want a drink after all. Mr. Heritage hasn't had any dinner.'

As they went towards Mandrake's table, heads turned to look at Paul. Hazel realized it was too much to hope for it to go unnoticed when a man was interviewed by the police in Steeple Tottering.

No sooner had they sat down than the manageress, whom Hazel had hitherto regarded as rather disagreeable, appeared as by magic, bearing a covered plate on a tray, placed it in front of Paul and removed the aluminium cover. On the plate reposed three hearteningly thick slices of nut-brown sirloin, five large richly brown roast potatoes and a number of flawlessly green Brussels sprouts.

'I heard you'd been delayed, Mr. Heritage,' she said, 'so I kept a cut back for you.'

When she had gone Hazel whispered, 'Was it all right?'

'I honestly wouldn't know,' said Paul. 'They asked about the fire first, where I'd been at the time it started; then they said some further information had come up about Lars and could I explain the telegram I'd sent after his death. I told them the truth, for what it was worth. Then they asked when I'd first met Mrs. Porsen—Angela—and I told them, this evening. I didn't get the impression that they believed me, but they're certain to interview her in the morning and she'll obviously bear me out.'

Hazel sat dumb. Mandrake said, 'Yes, about that, she will, but I wouldn't count on her much for anything else. She—er—seems to find the idea that you might have killed her husband for love of her rather flattering.'

Paul laid his knife and fork down and looked at Mandrake in amazement. 'I see,' he said at last.

'She would have been perfectly all right,' said Hazel bitterly, 'if you'd only left her to me and not butted in.'

'You'd hardly suppose I should sit there in silence while you beguiled the chief witness into embarking on the most blatant piece of lying.'

'Yes, I did,' said Hazel. 'I'd have done it for you.'

'She wouldn't have stuck to that story once she'd thought it over. It's better to know where you stand.'

Hazel didn't answer. Instead she turned to Paul.

'To-night, on the way down from the Toad, Peggy Wormwell boasted to the barmaid here that she'd had a part in the film.'

'Well, she hadn't. It was just a rather mean practical joke of Lars'.'

'I know. There was a rumour about it right at the start of the picture, but everyone in the unit denied it, and no more was said. So far as I know Peggy never mentioned it again, but to-night, while the hangar was burning, when there was no chance of anyone finding out it wasn't true, she did. Are you sure *she* knew there wasn't any film in the camera when Lars pretended to film her?'

'Not at the time. She really thought she was being filmed. And Wormwell must have thought so too. That was what the fuss was about after the rushes when you nearly got trampled underfoot. Her father wanted to strangle Lars.'

'Perhaps he did strangle Lars.'

'For pretending to film his daughter and not doing it? Oh, hardly.'

'Perhaps she'd paid in advance.'

'Paid what?'

'It's generally referred to as "his price." '

'You can't think he actually seduced her? No one saw them together except during the shooting and Lars certainly hadn't time for that, then.'

'Don't you remember my telling you I'd seen him out at Pennyfold at dusk, with his arm round a village girl?'

'You didn't say it was Peggy Wormwell.'

'It didn't seem important, then.'

'I see,' said Paul. 'Lars wouldn't waste any time looking for wild strawberries, would he? And you think Wormwell would be the type to avenge his daughter's honour? But would he have to burn the hangar?'

Hazel said, 'I'm not sure. I've been trying to think how he would react. Supposing, for instance, he caught her creeping in very late and dishevelled—it's my guess he'd beat her first and listen afterwards. Her reaction would be to say, "But father, I've been out with a film director and he's promised to get me in pictures." I wouldn't call him a sentimental type. He might consider it a reasonable exchange; a great many people do. Lars would take his fake shots and Wormwell would get on with his life, satisfied that his daughter was started on the road to fame. He'd boast a bit perhaps, and wait for the great day when the picture would be shown at the local cinema. At the rushes he'd realize what had happened; not only had his daughter been seduced but he'd been taken in and made a fool of. Mightn't he kill Lars as much for making a fool of them as for his daughter's virtue? And after that, when he realized that the picture's release would still make him and his daughter laughing-stocks, it wouldn't be very difficult for him to set fire to the hangar.'

'You say she told Connie on the way down from the Toad that she was in the picture?' asked Mandrake. 'Do you know if she mentioned it before they could see the hangar burning?'

'No,' said Hazel. 'I asked Connie that and she didn't seem sure one way or the other. Of course, if Peggy said something about it before they saw the hangar it would suggest she knew about the fire in advance—and that she or her father had something to do with it.'

'You seem to have thought quite a lot,' said Paul. 'How do we set about extracting the truth from Wormwell?'

Hazel looked harassed. 'I've got five weddings and two deaths to write up to-morrow morning.' she said, then brightening, 'I'll stay away from the office. I had a temperature on Sunday and I've never been in one position long enough for anyone to take it since then. I'll go and talk to Wormwell.'

'Someone would see you and tell your boss,' said Paul. 'Is there any reason why I shouldn't go?'

'Yes, you're a marked man already,' said Mandrake. 'Anything you do will be conspicuous. Far and away the simplest plan is for me to go on a little sketching expedition and chance to make a study of the Wormwell front door. People get so used to your being there that in a little while they bring you cups of tea and tell you *everything*.'

'I didn't,' said Hazel.

'You are a woman in a million,' admitted Mandrake. 'When I say "people," I am never referring to you. Can you see any flaws in my proposal?'

'I don't suppose so, except that I don't trust you.'

'I give you my word of honour I'll tell you everything that happens.'

'All right,' said Hazel.

Mandrake was finding the clutter of sheds and farm tools that constituted the view of Farmer Wormwell's front door more discouraging than he had foreseen. Wormwell himself had not appeared and a large and deadly-looking turkey had, several times. Mandrake had knocked on the door when he first arrived, but though the door was ajar no one had answered. Supposing that the household must be at the barns or feeding the chickens, he set up his easel, sketched in some outlines and began to match the tints of rust, dried mud, dung and weather-beaten brickwork which made up the prospect before him. Presently Wormwell or Peggy would appear, edge up behind his easel and say, 'Painting the porch, eh?' and then in an access of pride begin to tidy the porch, moving the rotting sacks or the hairless broom or the pieces of corrugated tin—all of which Mandrake had already included in his composition. Conversation would ensue and in a little while all would be revealed.

That was the plan; but an hour had passed and Mandrake's presence had gone unremarked except by the turkey which clearly took exception to it, and by a small pig which had nosed its way in and out of the front door, under the broomstick—bringing it down thwack on its back—and had then run squealing back the way it had come.

The sketch-pad was now covered with nondescript greys and browns all about the same depth of tone, and there didn't seem to be anything further he could do about it as a sketch. He toyed with the idea of adding the turkey cock, but either the thing would look like a turkey or it wouldn't look like a turkey, and there didn't seem very much to recommend either possibility. He decided to make an excursion round the farm.

As he stood up the door opened and Peggy came out with a pail of vegetable peelings and 'mash.' From both sides of the house pigs of all sizes converged, squealing, upon her, till it was all she could do to keep her balance. Ignoring this onslaught, Peggy pulled a bright-coloured handkerchief off her head with her free hand and came towards Mandrake.

'Good morning. Did you want father? Oh—painting?'

The pigs surged round her ankles. One of them sent the easel flying. Mandrake snatched the paintbox and held it above his head.

'Oh, your painting's gone over,' said Peggy, and putting down the pail stooped and picked up Mandrake's block. The pigs immediately upset the pail and began to consume the ensuing mess.

'Look at them,' said Peggy without unquiet, and turned back to Mandrake's sketch. 'Pretty, isn't it,' she hazarded. 'Pity there's a bit of mash on the corner.'

'It doesn't matter,' said Mandrake above the din. 'It wasn't very good.'

'Oh, *I* like it,' shrilled Peggy, used to making her voice heard above the pigs and unaware of any inconvenience. 'Be better if you had someone standing in the doorway.'

'I'm afraid I'm not very expert at human beings.'

'Oh, go on, just for a lark. Nobody'll see you. Dad's gone down to the village.' With one hand she was withdrawing the pins from her front curls and putting them in her pocket.

'I wasn't contemplating doing anything that your father mightn't see.'

'No, but it's more fun with him away, isn't it? Come on in and have a glass of fizzy lemonade. There's nothing else. Dad only drinks in the pub. He won't bring nothing home.'

'It would perhaps be quieter indoors,' agreed Mandrake, and picking up his satchel and easel he followed her inside the farmhouse. 'Will Mr. Wormwell be away long?' he asked, taking a rush-bottomed chair.

'I don't know. Did you want him? I could telephone for him. He's gone down to the "George." '

'Have you got a telephone out here?'

'Oh, yes. Father had to have the telephone. Something might happen to one of the animals. He worries about them.'

'Doesn't he worry about you?'

'Oh, well, you know what I mean. Animals cost money. He worries about money. That's what he's worrying about now, down at the "George." Trying to find someone to take responsibility for the hire of the sheep and that. He's afraid he mightn't get it now it's all been burnt down and Mr. Porsen dead.'

As she talked she continued to remove the pins from her curls. 'Was he expecting a lot?' asked Mandrake.

'Well, when first they spoke about it he didn't think it would be much anyway, so he said he'd settle just for the sheep to be mentioned and his name on the programme. But they wouldn't do that, and when he began to see how much money they had to waste in filming he didn't see why he shouldn't have some. He arranged quite a stiff price, so much per sheep per day, and so much for the man to look after them—that was father—and him to keep check and present his bill when it was all finished after the retakes and everything. Of course when he heard Mr. Porsen was dead he went straight down to the hangar and they told him not to worry, they'd be going on with the picture and it would probably mean more retakes and more money for Dad. Next thing he knows it's all gone up in smoke; no picture left; nothing to prove they ever even took any pictures of his sheep. If they like to try and duck out of it, it's easy.'

'I don't suppose they'll try and duck out of it.'

'Don't you? That's all you know. Film people'll duck out of anything.'

Mandrake looked interested and sympathetic. '*All* film people—or just one? Mr. Porsen certainly struck me as a slippery customer.'

'Are you telling me?' Against her better judgment Peggy was drawn. 'Promise you the earth, he would.'

'Money, do you mean?' Mandrake succeeded in keeping the excitement he felt out of his voice.

'No, not money, something far more important—a part in the picture.'

'And he never gave you a part?'

Peggy remembered her position. 'Yes,' she said. 'He did give me a part. I had to sing a little number, all by myself.'

'Whose idea was the number?'

'Mine. I've got a nice singing voice.'

'So you persuaded him to let you sing a number?'

'Me persuade him? Ha.'

'You mean he did the persuading and in consideration of your—being persuaded—he promised you should sing in the picture?'

'Something like that.'

'But you didn't sing in the picture.'

'Yes, I did. I sang, "How Deep is the Ocean?" '

'But it wasn't in the picture.'

'Yes, it was. I told you it was. That Gussie was at the camera and he said it came out lovely.'

'It didn't come out at all.'

'I tell you it did. Only you'll never see it now because the film's burnt.'

'There wasn't any film in the camera when he took it. I know there wasn't, so you needn't pretend. I'm not going to tell anybody. It's one of the meanest tricks I ever heard of.'

The sympathy was too much for her. 'It *was* mean, wasn't it? I wasn't half glad after that, when the film got burnt. Nobody'll have to know, now, that I wasn't in it.'

'Your father knew, though, didn't he? He saw the rushes. What did he think about it?'

'Dad was furious. Wanted to knock his block off

then and there, but all those technicians got in the way and got Mr. Porsen into an office. And when Dad said he had to see him, first they said he was engaged and would see him in a minute and then at last that Mercedes came and told him Mr. Porsen had left for the day and couldn't she take any message?

'Father went over to Bratton then and got drunk. He never gets drunk in his home town—and then he came home and beat me up. In the morning he wasn't able to get angry about it any more; he just said he might as well put it on the bill as another twenty-five sheep for two days and he didn't suppose Mr. Porsen would have the face to query it. That's why it's so awkward him being dead because someone else might.'

Mandrake's growing conviction that Wormwell was innocent became certainty. No one who balanced his daughter's virtue against the hire of twenty-five sheep for two days would be likely to avenge it in blood. He had pursued a red herring and had no more time to waste.

'Well, thank you very much,' he said, getting to his feet and beginning to collect his equipment. 'It's been a most enjoyable conversation.'

Peggy looked betrayed. Her head was now a mass of tight, tortured little curls and her lips were like patent leather. 'Aren't you going to paint me?' she said. 'I thought you came in for that.'

'But I told you I wasn't any good at human beings,' Mandrake protested.

'But I said "Oh, go on, just for a lark," and you came in. I've taken out my curlers.' The disappointment on her face was heartrending. Life, fame and Lars had failed her all in a few days; could art and Mandrake add the final drop to her cup of disillusion?

For his part Mandrake couldn't. Out of the goodness of his heart he sat down to paint Peggy Wormwell.

12

Oft' have I seen a skilful angler try
The various colours of the treach'rous fly.

JOHN GAY

GOODNESS ought to be rewarded and, in this case,
it was. In no time at all Mandrake realized he
couldn't manage the curls. 'Just a moment,'
he said, hand poised over the fresh sheet of paper.
'You don't look right, somehow. Weren't you
wearing a bandana on your head when you first
came out?'

Peggy's face fell. 'Yes, I had my headsquare on but
I've taken it off.'

'Put it on again,' said Mandrake relentlessly. 'Knot
it under your chin.' Reluctantly she tied it on. Mandrake began to draw, and as he did he began to be
aware that he had seen the handkerchief before.

The colours were as garish as Peggy could desire, but
the material was dull and soft and certainly pure silk.
It was a little too small for her purpose. The corners
barely knotted under her chin. Clearly it had started
life as a man's pocket handkerchief, the possession of a
man of means though not necessarily of taste, for the

design was hideous enough. Mandrake's apathy had departed and he fervently sketched in the outlines.

Now he reached for his colour box. 'Take your make-up off,' he commanded.

Peggy whimpered.

'You've never sat to an artist before, have you?' he asked coldly, and, demoralized, she groped in her pocket for a crumpled scrap of cotton and polished her face till it shone.

'She is stripped of her armour,' he thought. 'Her morale is gone. She'll tell me the truth, poor child.' He mixed a wash of pale umber and began to apply it all over the face and neck of his drawing.

'That's a nice handkerchief,' he said.

'Do you like it?'

'Yes. I could do with one like that. Will you sell it to me?'

'If you like.'

'Half a crown?'

'All right, if you like.'

So she didn't value it, thought Mandrake. It must have cost at least a guinea. But had Lars given it to her or was it the one that Paul had seen Lars spreading on the grass before he went to sleep near the Toad, and which had disappeared such a little while after, before Mandrake had picked up the matches? For he was sure he had seen it in Lars' breast pocket at some time.

'Won't your father ask what's happened to it?'

'No, why should he?'

'Didn't he bring it home to you?'

'Him? He doesn't give me things.'

'Who did then? Or did you buy it?'

'This? Oh, I got it at Woolworth's.'

'Oh no, you didn't. That's a French silk handkerchief and they don't have them in Woolworth's.' Mandrake was on his feet now, bolstering his bluff with the weight and size of his person. His eyes bored into and through her. All friendliness was wiped from his face. 'You stole it,' he said.

'No, I didn't. I never did.'

'Tell me the truth then and I'll believe you,' said Mandrake, still towering over her.

'I found it,' said Peggy dispiritedly. 'As if you'll believe that.'

'I'll believe it. Where?'

'In the Widdle.'

'I beg your pardon?'

'The Widdle. It's a stream that runs down from above Littledown into the Sallow. You must have come over it by the bridge as you came up from Steeple Tottering.'

Mandrake sat down and picked up his brush. 'I did come over a bridge.'

'Well, that's the Widdle underneath it.'

'And you found it in the stream?'

'Yes, just by the bridge.'

'When?'

'Saturday night.'

'What time?'

'Oh—about ten, I s'pose—could have been later.'

'It must have been pitch dark.'

'It wasn't *very* dark.'

'Whatever were you doing fishing in the middle of the night?'

'I wasn't. Somebody threw it away and my friend fished it out.'

'Who threw it away?'

'I don't know. I never saw them.'

'I think you'd better be a bit more explicit if you want me to believe you.'

'What's that?'

'Explain more fully.'

'Well, we were under the bridge, if you want to know.'

'We?'

'Oh, me and a chap.'

'In the water?'

'No. There's quite a wide bank at the side under the bridge. It's nice there.'

'And private?'

'We weren't doing anything. This fellow I'd been out with said he'd walk back home with me and we stopped under the bridge to say good night. While we was there we heard someone's footsteps crunching over the bridge and a little bundle came over and splashed into the water. Scared the life out of me. We didn't know what it was. Then the chap I was with lit a match and we could see the colours just under the water. He fished it out, and it was this handkerchief with a stone tied inside it. There was nothing wrong with it, so he gave it to me.'

'And you don't know who threw it?'

'A drunk, I s'pose, on his way home.'

'Was your father drunk that night?'

'No, he was waiting for me when I got back, stone cold sober.'

'Did you mention it to him?'

'No, why should I?'

'Has he seen it?'

'Yes. I pressed it out and had it round my neck on Sunday.'

'Did he like it?'

'He didn't say anything. He never notices what I wear.'

Mandrake's portrait wasn't very nice. He'd had several tries at the nose and the eyes weren't both looking in quite the same direction. Some of the green of the bandana had run down into the forehead. He decided that as Peggy was the only person to whom the painting could have any value he might as well give it to her. In the circumstances he added a generous helping of vermilion to the cheeks and mouth.

'Where does this road go to, besides this farm?' he asked.

'There's about six cottages up along and then nothing for the next five miles till you get to Watchett and Bratton.'

'Thank you,' said Mandrake, wiping his palette with his rag and beginning to fold up his paintbox. He felt that he would prefer to hand her the picture at the very last moment and not wait to see the expression on her face when she looked at it. 'Now would you like to sell me the handkerchief or not? It's just as you like. I'm satisfied that you found it quite legitimately.'

'All right,' she said, 'I don't mind.'

Mandrake handed her the half-crown and she pulled the square of silk off her curls and gave it to him. He collected his materials and detached the top sheet from the sketching block. 'Good day,' he said. 'And thank you. I shall be delighted if you will accept this with my compliments.' He laid the still damp water-colour on the table and went through the doorway surprisingly quickly. Peggy's cries of delight and gratitude followed him out into the yard. Art was in the eyes of the beholder.

Mandrake found Paul in his room at the 'George.' He said, 'You remember telling us that the last glimpse you had of Lars was when he was spreading a coloured handkerchief on the grass?'

'Yes.'

'Well, no coloured handkerchief was found either on the grass or in the dead man's pockets.'

'Wasn't it?'

'Not by me, and I have to admit I looked, in a general way, in all those places. Would you remember the handkerchief if you saw it?'

'I can't say.'

Mandrake spread his trophy on the bed.

'That was it,' said Paul. 'So Wormwell had it?'

'I'm afraid not,' said Mandrake. 'I fancy the murderer stuffed it in his pocket and, later, realizing it might implicate him, threw it away.'

'So you don't know who it was?'

'Not yet,' said Mandrake, 'not yet. Don't be impatient. The mills of God grind slowly, but it is a widely held theory that they grind exceeding small.'

'I hadn't realized that you regarded yourself as one of them,' said Paul. 'Have you established whether it might have been thrown away by me?'

'Not conclusively. Do you happen to have an alibi for between ten and eleven on the Saturday night that Lars died?'

'So far as I remember I went out for a walk by myself. Is it important?'

'I shall know in a little while,' said Mandrake cheerfully and departed in the direction of the *Sallowshire Guardian*.

Hazel was alone in the Junior Reporters, typing for dear life. To-day was Wednesday and market day in Steeple Tottering. It was also zero hour for the main features of the weekly. Maisie who got lightheaded over punctuation on an empty stomach had perforce been sent out for the first lunch. Hazel's turn was due on her return, but often on Wednesday she missed lunch altogether. Lightbody had an instinct for bundling last-minute copy on to her and trusting her professional pride would triumph over hunger. Usually it did.

Hazel looked up at the end of a paragraph to find Mandrake padding into the office.

'Oh,' she said with something like a moan of relief. 'It's you. Thank heavens. You've been ages.'

'It was heavier going than I anticipated. I'm afraid they didn't do it.'

'Oh, dear.' Hazel looked defeated. 'Are you sure?'

'When Wormwell found that Lars had—defaulted—

on his daughter he decided to charge him for an extra twenty-five sheep for two days, in lieu, one can but gather, of his daughter's virtue. That is the act of a practical man. If he had intended to put an end to Lars' life he would have waited till the bill had been paid.'

'I suppose so.' She looked disheartened and bewildered. 'So what do we do now?'

'Let me see the files of your newspaper, just the last few weeks. There's something I read but I'm not sure I remember correctly.'

Hazel handed him the huge strawboard folder from its shelf. He flicked through the pages until his eye came to rest on a column, then he grunted a couple of times and snapped it shut. 'I'm a half-witted fool,' he growled suddenly. 'A film and its director are suddenly destroyed and I search for personal motives, instead of having the sense to study the script and find out what that contained that might germinate its own destruction. I shall have to read the script.'

'You can't do that,' protested Hazel. 'Nobody can *read* a film-script. They're like legal documents. They get you so befuddled with their especial jargon that you're in a stupor before you get to the point.'

'Then we will read it together,' said Mandrake, 'over a great deal of black coffee, taking it in turns so that one of us is always on the alert to detect any signs of the "snow sleep" creeping over the other. Come along.'

'I've read the book that the film was based on.'

'So have I. It is the script we require.'

'I've got to wait for Maisie in case the telephone rings.'

'When is she due?'

'Five minutes ago.'

'Where is she?'

'In the China Dog café on the corner.'

'Then lock the door, take your key in your hand and lay it on the table before her. She will recognize that you mean business and have more respect for you in future. If you apprehend a murderer in time for the weekly issue, the paper will hardly be in a position to quibble about five minutes.'

'Do you think we shall?' asked Hazel doubtfully, albeit doing as she was told. 'It seems a very slow way to set about it.'

Mandrake decided not to mention the mills of God twice in the same morning. Hazel routed Maisie out of the 'Ladies' in the China Dog, and then, with Mandrake, set out through the thronged, market-day street for the 'George.'

They met Hollinshead in the lounge. He was willing enough to help them to borrow a script but his own had perished in the fire. Gussie's was somewhere in his room, but had been mislaid. He had looked for it that morning and not found it. He volunteered to look again. Not having spoken to Mercedes since the session in the bramble patch, Hazel suggested Mandrake should approach her. Mercedes explained that all the spares had gone up in smoke, but that each member of the unit had his or her own copy, which they naturally kept safely in their rooms. Her own copy was, of course, in her dispatch case under her bed. She could not part with it, though she was willing for Mandrake to glance through it in her presence. As she went upstairs to get it, Coram McCoram passed through the lounge. Hazel approached him. He assured her he'd have been delighted to let her read his script, only he'd lent it to someone. Just for the moment he couldn't think whom.

Gussie came downstairs and said he was terribly sorry, it couldn't have been in his room after all. Hazel and Mandrake went upstairs. Mercedes' door was open and, whitefaced, she was going through her belongings. She looked up as Mandrake stood in the doorway. 'It isn't there,' she said. 'I know it was there. It's gone . . .'

They asked Bertrand and Paul and even Angela, but not one copy could they discover of the script of 'Petronella.' Everyone had lent theirs, or mislaid it or just put it down and it had vanished. At last they met Elizabeth coming along the passage from the bathroom.

'Now, isn't that too bad,' she said when they asked her. 'I've just lent it to that dear little Orlando. He said he wanted to check up about something—as if it mattered, poor sweet—it'll never be made now—not that I would want to be the one to tell him. . . .'

But Mandrake and Hazel were already half-way down the stairs.

13

Fast, fast through town and hamlet
The Smart Detectives flew——
CHOLMONDELEY PENNELL

'WHATEVER is happening in this town?' snapped
Mandrake as they emerged into the street in
the middle of a flock of sheep.

'It's market day,' said Hazel. 'Didn't you know.'

'Yes, I suppose I did. It doesn't matter, anyway.
Now, as we go, perhaps you can suggest some legitimate business upon which a man might chance to call
at the offices of the Catchment Board.'

'Won't it do to say you want to borrow the script
back?'

'It might, and it might not. Now I am one who
favours the oblique approach in these things. It——'

'Takes so much longer?' suggested Hazel.

'I hope you underrate me,' said Mandrake mildly.
'The direct approach might slow things down even
more disastrously.'

'Then try telling him you want to take a boat from
the upper reaches of the Sallow as far as Watling
Willows, and you need advice about depth and navig-
ability. Will that do?'

'Admirably,' said Mandrake. 'I can't think what I should do without you.'

'What did you have to look for in my files?'

'I seemed to remember reading an article which mentioned that a leading citizen had lived all his life at Littledown. Not many people live at Littledown. I had to be sure I was right.'

'Orlando,' said Hazel. 'I wrote that column myself.'

'That rather belatedly turned my thoughts to the film script—and our abortive pursuit of the film script turned our thoughts back inevitably to Orlando. And here we are.'

Hazel felt that something must be missing from his reported train of thought but had to admit that they were outside the office of the Catchment Board. The door was closed. Mandrake tried the handle and then thumped on the door.

'It's his lunch hour, too,' Hazel reminded him.

Mandrake shied away from a couple of apprehensive bullocks that were being driven away from market. When they had passed Hazel said, 'Mr. Hallam usually lunches at the China Dog.'

'I don't think he's there to-day,' said Mandrake.

'Why ever not?'

'As we came from the "George" I noticed a curl of smoke coming from the chimney of this building,' said Mandrake. 'Not a steady puff, just a wisp, and then another wisp. It seemed odd that anyone should require a fire on one of the hottest days of summer, but on the other hand there must have been quite a lot of paper.'

'Paper?'

'Yes. I would like to identify it before it is too late.'

'The scripts?' said Hazel. 'You mean he's burning the scripts?'

Mandrake had been trying to peer in through the window but a khaki lace curtain obscured all possible view of the interior. He moved round the corner of the building and a little way down the narrow alley that separated it from the harness-makers on its left. On the level of Mandrake's nose was a narrow sill and above it a narrow window into which he could not see. He put his hands on the high sill and, with a terrific spring, raised himself so that he got a momentary glimpse into the office, and dropped to the pavement.

'He's there,' he said, 'bending over the grate at the back of the room, feeding foolscap into it for dear life.'

He rapped sharply on the window with his knuckles. No sound or sign came from within.

'He's determined to get them all burnt before he opens the door again,' said Hazel. 'After all, he's entitled to keep it shut. The office *is* closed. However are we going to get in?'

'Like this.' Mandrake withdrew from his pocket a florid silk handkerchief, shook it out and held it by its two corners, then he turned to look at the road. 'I require,' he said, 'a missile. A stone would do,' he added magnanimously, stepping back and studying the gutter's length.

But missiles, or even stones, were not so readily come by. Apart from a few recent horse-droppings nothing presented itself. Mandrake gave up and decided to sacrifice his pocket-knife. He knotted it into the hand-kerchief and threw it sharply through the window with a tinkle of breaking glass.

The result was magical. In a matter of moments the front door was silently opened and Orlando stood on the threshold.

'You wished to see me?' he asked, gravely courteous. 'Will you come inside?' He stood aside for Mandrake. 'Ah, Hazel.'

Hazel followed Mandrake into the office, feeling perfectly miserable.

Hallam placed chairs for them both, and then, taking his own position between them and the fire, put the tips of his fingers together with an air of awaiting their pleasure. In the corner of the room the papers still smouldered in the grate. A small hole gaped in the window, but the handkerchief containing the missile was nowhere to be seen.

'A warm day,' Mandrake began.

'It is indeed, too warm by half for the task I had in hand.'

'Is that so?'

'I was burning a quantity of outdated office corre-spondence. A filing system is an admirable thing in theory, but I find that in practice much goes in while nothing ever comes out. No one cares to take the personal responsibility of throwing anything away. So once every few months when I'm feeling energetic I go through the files myself and destroy the redundant matter.'

'A most praiseworthy undertaking.'

Hazel began to fear that this dignified exchange would continue until the papers were ashes and not a shred of evidence remained to show what they had been, yet the atmosphere remained courtly and courteous and it seemed that nothing could shatter it.

The flames had died down to nothing. Hallam picked up the poker. 'Even paper, however, needs constant encouragement to burn, otherwise it excludes the necessary air and the flame goes out.' He leaned forward and stirred the pages with his poker. As he did so, he silently added a scarlet and green handkerchief to the resultant blaze.

Hazel was on her feet, but Mandrake was there before her. He had closed with Hallam and twisted the poker from his hand. As it clattered to the floor Hazel picked it up and raked the handkerchief on to the floor and stamped out the flames. Then she snatched out some pages of foolscap and stamped on them too. Hallam sank back into his swivel chair, panting like a man who had been running, but he didn't speak.

'It's the script of "Petronella," ' Hazel said. 'You were burning it.'

'Was I?' said Hallam, making a desperate effort at composure. 'Was I indeed? Dear me. There were some loose sheets in the office. They must have got into the discarded pile by mistake.'

'The same mistake,' said Mandrake, 'that has wiped out every copy of the script, every scrap of film and the director of the picture; the mistake, if I may say so, of a very thorough man.' As Mandrake towered over Hallam like a doom, he dropped his voice to a whisper.

'Not, however, so thorough as to avoid being seen and identified on the bridge when you threw away the dead man's handkerchief a few hours after his murder.'

Hallam's face was grey. He swallowed and opened his mouth, but no sound came out of it. A sudden collapse of the papers in the grate sent out a puff of fluttering blackened scraps of paper. Hallam took a gasping breath.

'What makes you think I would destroy the thing I had worked for?'

'I was going to suggest that you should tell us that. We have established beyond a shadow of doubt how and by whom Lars Porsen was murdered and his handiwork destroyed, but I am bound to admit to a certain curiosity as to why. It should prove a relief to you to make your reasons clear to sympathetic listeners while you still may.'

'Should it?' Hallam's eyes went from Mandrake to the papers in Hazel's hand, then to the florid half-burnt handkerchief and the splinters of glass on the floor. He seemed to shrink.

'Yes,' he said at last. 'Yes, indeed you are right. It has been a period of considerable strain.' He pressed his lips together, moistened them with his tongue, then passed his hands across his temples as though to try and relieve them of a solid compressing band. 'I have not been to sleep since, I believe, Friday—no, no, Thursday night of last week.'

'What happened on Friday?'

'Friday?' said Hallam, looking past him through the window. 'Friday?'

'Never mind Friday,' suggested Mandrake. 'Begin at the beginning.'

Hallam continued to gaze out of the dusty window. 'The beginning was a long time ago,' he said, 'perhaps two hundred years, when a peasant girl was found to have miraculous powers.'

A smile of ineffable sadness touched his features and Hazel recognized how frail he was and that he was older than she had suspected. The smile faded as he spoke again. 'Petronella loved nature and her sheep and her Maker, and was in love with no man; she was neither coy nor coquettish and was probably not technically beautiful, but she had the simplicity of absolute goodness and the serenity of absolute purity. She did not ask for her tale to be told. It was I who uncovered it and blunderingly revealed it to the world.' Now he spoke quickly and protestingly. 'But I did it for love. I did it with reverence. It was my justification; the consummation of my life.'

'You did it very well,' said Mandrake quietly. 'I have read your story.'

Orlando seemed not to hear. 'I am not, nor have I ever sought to be, a writer,' he continued, 'but I told the facts straightforwardly in the purest language I could utter, and, being sincere, it was enough. When it was done I sent it to a publisher of the highest reputation, and when I learned that he wished to publish it and was willing to hazard an advance payment of thirty pounds I was most proud. It had been in every sense a labour of love and payment had never been my objective. When a cinematograph company offered two thousand pounds for a licence to make a moving picture, my instinct was to refuse. But my sister, who was then living, reasoned that for Petronella's story to be more widely known must have an uplifting effect on at least a few and, recalling the violence and tawdriness so often glorified on the nation's cinema screens, we decided that to replace such offerings, even for one week out of many, with this story of simple goodness, could not be wrong.

'It was arranged by post and I had no idea when or by whom the picture would be made. When I encountered Mr. Porsen in the train, and learned who he was, even though I was astonished by his apparent crudity, I yet felt that for a story so unworldly to have commended itself to him, he must have qualities of perception that did not appear on the surface, or how had he the vision to wish to make this film at all? It never occurred to me that anyone capable of appreciating the story should wish to debase it into a vehicle for a series of star performances in situations suggested by, yet in no way spiritually resembling, the circumstances of my story. I was, after all, a child in this medium, and only knew that other films had, at times, come from this extraordinary machine which have moved men to awe and wonder. And perhaps I expected a miracle. Petronella had done miracles before. . . .'

Hallam's voice had sunk to a whisper and his gaze was concentrated on something quite outside the vision of Hazel and Mandrake. Then his pupils dilated and he winced sharply and wiped his hand across his eyes.

'Only when I saw those rushes on Friday did I know

without a vestige of hope that no miracle had happened
or could happen; that I had sent 'my darling to the
lions,' and that I had been paid for it. I wrestled all
night with the problem, then I took my money in my
hand and went with it to Lars Porsen to buy back my
story. He laughed in my face. Two thousand . . . they
had spent tens of thousands already and were committed to infinitely more. . . . And the picture was going
to be a success. Was I mad? Didn't I know when I was
well off? I should be made. I should be able to ask my
own figure for the next. . . . As if there could ever be a
next. . . .

'I walked for miles, trying to think what I should do.
I had tried the honourable course and been refused. I
prayed for an accident to remove this indefatigable
destroyer, for a thunderbolt to fall, but no such thing
came. No accident would overtake him. Mine was the
sin and mine must be its undoing. I found that I was
approaching Petronella's pool, feeling, half-consciously,
that somehow she would give me the solution if I could
get near to the place where she had lived. But the sun
shone and the brook sparkled and I could only find
that I had defiled it; that its purity was for evermore
sullied and the price was two thousand pounds.

'I found myself turning away and going on up the
Pennyfold Road till I came to the Roman Barrow. In
the sunlit hollow between the Barrow and the Toad
Rock I saw Lars Porsen, lying on the grass. At first I
thought, 'He is dead. It has happened,' and I wanted
to shout aloud and fall down on my knees in praise.
Then he moved and grunted like a pig in the sun and

I knew that *it had not happened yet*. And I knew why I had come.

'I knelt on the grass, put my fingers round his neck with both thumbs on the carotid arteries and pressed. He struggled, but my strength was not the strength of man and he stopped struggling very soon. I rolled him to the edge of the cliff and pushed him over just below the Toad. I did not watch him fall. As I crossed the grass towards the road I saw that his handkerchief still lay where he had been sleeping.

'I decided to throw it after him but as I again approached the drop I saw what I had not seen before —a man sketching on the ground below. As I watched he began to stand up. I turned and hurried out of sight and on down the hill, forgetting the handkerchief which I later found I had put into my pocket. I returned to my office and tidied myself. On the calendar I found a note that I was to go to Miss Brentbridge's party at the "George" Hotel. I went to the party.'

Mandrake leaned forward. 'But his tie,' he said. 'You must have tied it on again before you rolled him over.'

'Nothing of the sort,' said Hallam. 'His tie was on all the time. He had loosened it a little, that was all. During the evening I realized I had the handkerchief, and so, on my way home, I tied a stone in it, as you know, and threw it into the Widdle. That was a mistake. I of all people should have taken thought that the Widdle at that point is neither deep enough nor swift enough to offer a permanent hiding-place for anything, but I didn't think of that, then. I had supposed that after the inquest everyone would go away and peace would return as though the hideous film project had never been, but nothing is ever as simple as all that. I was asked to a luncheon party by the young man, Rupert Rollo, and there to my distress I heard them discussing the continuation of the picture under a new director. What I had done would be worthless unless I could also encompass the destruction of every piece of film and every single script that had ever existed of this travesty.

'The fire at the hangar was easy. It stood by itself in a field, some distance from any habitation. I secreted the petrol before the unit cars left for the ceremony at the Rock. The building was unattended. I was able to make my preparations without panic or hurry so that the result was an unqualified success. Tracing and acquiring every copy of the script was considerably more hazardous, but in most cases I managed to abstract them from bedrooms while the occupants were at meals. In one or two cases I had to ask outright for the loan of a script on some pretext or other, but naturally this would not have been an advisable course on too many occasions. I was, however, successful. Those crumpled fragments in Miss Fairweather's hands are the only surviving relics of what I understand was to have been described as "A Film Epic of All Time." '

Hallam leaned back a little in his swivel chair. 'You know it is rather a relief to have been found out. I hadn't really made any plans for afterwards.' He smiled half apologetically. 'Do you mind if *I* make the telephone call to the police?'

'I should be unspeakably relieved,' said Mandrake. Hallam stretched his hand towards the telephone.

'Mr. Hallam,' said Hazel, 'please don't think I ever imagined it could have been you. I only tried to find out who it was because the police seemed to think it must be Paul.'

'Paul?' His hand stayed in mid-action.

'Paul Heritage, the art director.'

'Ah, I know the one you mean. A most agreeable young man. Oh, no, no, that would have been a pity.'

Hallam's fingers closed over the telephone receiver and his other hand began to dial the number of the police station.

In the street they met Angela. 'Tell me,' she cried, 'there's a rumour. People saw the police go into that office and you come out. . . . What has really happened?'

'The murderer,' said Mandrake, 'has confessed.'

'But who? Oh, you must see I ought to know.'

Mandrake turned to Hazel. 'Do you want to keep this exclusive?'

'I couldn't if I tried. Everyone will know in no time. It's Orlando Hallam,' she said to Angela.

'Then not Paul? Oh, I'm so relieved it isn't Paul. Such a sweet nature I never could believe it whatever they said. Of course I've had to avoid him since yesterday because it would have made it look worse for him if we'd seemed too friendly.'

A sudden, determined look came over her features. '*I* must be the first to tell him. Dear Paul, the relief will be so enormous.'

'Hazel's going to tell him,' Mandrake almost shouted. 'Why you practically put the rope round his neck yourself.'

'I? Oh, professor, I haven't the remotest idea what you're talking about.' She dismissed the quibble and went on eagerly, 'I feel sure it will come best from me—as Lars' wife you know,' she added with splendid lack of reasonableness. 'I'm so happy for him.' With a warm pressure of the hand to both Mandrake and Hazel she was gone down the street towards the 'George.'

'Shall we run?' asked Mandrake, hurrying Hazel along the pavement.

'I don't think so,' said Hazel. 'I should probably lose if I did.'

'But I want to see fair play,' he protested. 'He's only a lad and she's a consummate artist. He might not be able to stand up to her technique. She's a single lady now, we must remember.'

'I had thought of that.'

'From the look of it, so has she, otherwise why hasn't she gone back to her rehearsal? The police had finished questioning her quite early this morning. You didn't save him for her, did you?'

'If I had anything to do with saving him, I did it for him. Anyway, I ought to be at the office.'

'You've had nothing to eat.'

'Never mind.'

'I do mind. I've had nothing to eat myself. Come back to the "George" and eat a quick sandwich with me in the bar. There'll be nothing left worth having anywhere else.'

He gave her no chance to argue but steered her firmly into the 'George.' Already the rumour was spreading. Connie welcomed them like heroes and offered to cut fresh sandwiches. The bar filled up miraculously. They were offered drinks. They were asked details.

'There's one thing I'd like to have settled,' said Hazel, rather surprised to find herself addressing so large a throng, 'and that is how the average man ties his tie.'

'How do you mean?' someone asked.

'Well, if one or two of you wouldn't mind untying your ties and tying them afresh, it would settle a point that has been bothering Professor Mandrake.'

Seven willing pairs of hands unleashed seven ties and then retied them. Four passed the right end over the left, three the left over the right. Hazel said, 'Thank you. Are any of you gentlemen left-handed?'

No one was. Hazel avoided Mandrake's eye and smiled her appreciation. 'Now, if you can persuade him, I daresay the Professor will tell you the whole story of his capture,' she said. 'It wasn't really my doing at all.'

The group moved in round Mandrake. From the corner of her eye Hazel saw Angela coming downstairs in her outdoor things, followed by a porter with a suitcase. Looking neither to right nor left she swept to the reception desk and asked to be given her bill. Hazel realized that Paul was standing at her elbow. She stood up with her sandwich in her hand. Paul took her by the other wrist and led her into the street.

'Is it true?' he said.

'Yes. Orlando confessed.'

'Poor devil,' said Paul. They walked in silence along the crowded street, Paul's fingers on her wrist. Presently he said, 'I've got to talk to you.'

'Yes,' replied Hazel, bemused.

'What do you mean, yes? Did you know all along?'

'No. I don't know anything.'

'Then why are you gazing at me with a wild surmise again?'

'I'm not,' said Hazel, and took a bite of her sandwich to show her nonchalance. She went on, a little muffled, 'I needn't look at you at all in future and then the question won't arise.'

A sheep broke out of the huddle that was being driven away from market by its purchaser and dashed between them closely followed by several more. 'I see there is to be a determinedly rural note in all our wooing,' said Paul.

'All our what?'

'Didn't you hear?'

'I'm not sure. I wouldn't want to make any mistake.'

'Shall I say it again?'

'Yes, please.'

But he didn't have the chance. Mr. Lightbody had emerged through the open door of the *Sallowshire Guardian* office and crossed the road as though shot by a gun.

'Hazel!' His hand fastened on her arm. 'Thank goodness I've found you. They tell me you've got the inside story. I've got a line open to Head Office. If you get on the 'phone right away we'll make the front page with a banner headline for the Pegasus mystery. I'll take your

sandwich.' He had one arm round her and was shep-
herding her through the market-day traffic as though
she were export porcelain. 'It's the biggest story of the
year and right on our doorstep. They'll have to increase
the weekly edition for this.'

At the kerb she managed to throw off his grip and
turned. Paul stood on the opposite pavement. A tractor,
two vans, and a herd of unhappy heifers separated
them. Paul took a breath and put both hands round
his mouth but his words were blotted out by the
concerted squeals of a netted cartload of pigs. Then
she couldn't even see him. Lightbody's hand gripped
her again. 'The line's open,' he said. 'We haven't a
moment to lose.' He propelled her into the office.

As Hazel bowed to the inevitable and picked up the
receiver, Lightbody bolted the door. 'I don't care who
comes, we'll have no interruptions for the next fifteen
minutes.'

Hazel lifted her eyes to the window which had been
polished that morning till it shone, as it always was on
market day. Outside her glass prison people came and
went in the sunlight along the pavement. She saw their
shapes passing and one shape that stopped. Paul's face
looked in till he saw her. He watched her a moment
then he breathed on the shining glass. With a deliberate
forefinger he wrote in capitals, across the misted surface,
his message which Hazel had to read backwards:

ᑌOY ƎVO⅃ I

Then Hazel began to dictate.

THE PERENNIAL LIBRARY MYSTERY SERIES

E. C. Bentley

TRENT'S LAST CASE
"One of the three best detective stories ever written."

—Agatha Christie

TRENT'S OWN CASE
"I won't waste time saying that the plot is sound and the detection satisfying. Trent has not altered a scrap and reappears with all his old humor and charm."   —Dorothy L. Sayers

Gavin Black

A DRAGON FOR CHRISTMAS
"Potent excitement!"   —New York Herald Tribune

THE EYES AROUND ME
"I stayed up until all hours last night reading *The Eyes Around Me,* which is something I do not do very often, but I was so intrigued by the ingeniousness of Mr. Black's plotting and the witty way in which he spins his mystery. I can only say that I enjoyed the book enormously."

—F. van Wyck Mason

YOU WANT TO DIE, JOHNNY?
"Gavin Black doesn't just develop a pressure plot in suspense, he adds uninfected wit, character, charm, and sharp knowledge of the Far East to make rereading as keen as the first race-through."   —Book Week

Nicholas Blake

THE BEAST MUST DIE
"It remains one more proof that in the hands of a really first-class writer the detective novel can safely challenge comparison with any other variety of fiction."   —The Manchester Guardian

THE CORPSE IN THE SNOWMAN
"If there is a distinction between the novel and the detective story (which we do not admit), then this book deserves a high place in both categories."   —The New York Times

THE DREADFUL HOLLOW
"Pace unhurried, characters excellent, reasoning solid."

—San Francisco Chronicle

Nicholas Blake (cont'd)

END OF CHAPTER
". . . admirably solid . . . an adroit formal detective puzzle backed up by firm characterization and a knowing picture of London publishing."
—*The New York Times*

HEAD OF A TRAVELER
"Another grade A detective story of the right old jigsaw persuasion."
—*New York Herald Tribune Book Review*

MINUTE FOR MURDER
"An outstanding mystery novel. Mr. Blake's writing is a delight in itself."
—*The New York Times*

THE MORNING AFTER DEATH
"One of Blake's best."
—Rex Warner

A PENKNIFE IN MY HEART
"Style brilliant . . . and suspenseful."
—*San Francisco Chronicle*

THE PRIVATE WOUND
[Blake's] best novel in a dozen years . . . . An intensely penetrating study of sexual passion . . . . A powerful story of murder and its aftermath."
—Anthony Boucher, *The New York Times*

A QUESTION OF PROOF
"The characters in this story are unusually well drawn, and the suspense is well sustained."
—*The New York Times*

THE SAD VARIETY
"It is a stunner. I read it instead of eating, instead of sleeping."
—Dorothy Salisbury Davis

THERE'S TROUBLE BREWING
"Nigel Strangeways is a puzzling mixture of simplicity and penetration, but all the more real for that."
—*The Times Literary Supplement*

THOU SHELL OF DEATH
"It has all the virtues of culture, intelligence and sensibility that the most exacting connoisseur could ask of detective fiction."
—*The Times* [London] *Literary Supplement*

THE WHISPER IN THE GLOOM
"One of the most entertaining suspense-pursuit novels in many seasons."
—*The New York Times*

Nicholas Blake (cont'd)

THE WIDOW'S CRUISE
"A stirring suspense. . . . The thrilling tale leaves nothing to be desired."
—*Springfield Republican*

THE WORM OF DEATH
"It [The Worm of Death] is one of Blake's very best—and his best is better than almost anyone's."　　　　　　—Louis Untermeyer

John & Emery Bonett

A BANNER FOR PEGASUS
"A gem! Beautifully plotted and set. . . . Not only is the murder adroit and deserved, and the detection competent, but the love story is charming."　　　　　—Jacques Barzun and Wendell Hertig Taylor

DEAD LION
"A clever plot, authentic background and interesting characters highly recommended this one."　　　　　　　　　　—*New Republic*

Christianna Brand

GREEN FOR DANGER
"You have to reach for the greatest of Great Names (Christie, Carr, Queen . . .) to find Brand's rivals in the devious subtleties of the trade."
—Anthony Boucher

TOUR DE FORCE (*available 3/82*)
"Complete with traps for the over-ingenious, a double-reverse surprise ending and a key clue planted so fairly and obviously that you completely overlook it. If that's your idea of perfect entertainment, then seize at once upon *Tour de Force.*"　　—Anthony Boucher, *The New York Times*

Marjorie Carleton

VANISHED
"Exceptional . . . a minor triumph."
—Jacques Barzun and Wendell Hertig Taylor, *A Catalogue of Crime*

George Harmon Coxe

MURDER WITH PICTURES
"[Coxe] has hit the bull's-eye with his first shot."
—*The New York Times*

Edmund Crispin

BURIED FOR PLEASURE
"Absolute and unalloyed delight."

—Anthony Boucher, *The New York Times*

D. M. Devine

MY BROTHER'S KILLER
"A most enjoyable crime story which I enjoyed reading down to the last moment." —Agatha Christie

Kenneth Fearing

THE BIG CLOCK
"It will be some time before chill-hungry clients meet again so rare a compound of irony, satire, and icy-fingered narrative. *The Big Clock* is . . . a psychothriller you won't put down." —*Weekly Book Review*

Andrew Garve

THE ASHES OF LODA
"Garve . . . embellishes a fine fast adventure story with a more credible picture of the U.S.S.R. than is offered in most thrillers."

—*The New York Times Book Review*

THE CUCKOO LINE AFFAIR
". . . an agreeable and ingenious piece of work." —*The New Yorker*

A HERO FOR LEANDA
"One can trust Mr. Garve to put a fresh twist to any situation, and the ending is really a lovely surprise." —*The Manchester Guardian*

MURDER THROUGH THE LOOKING GLASS
". . . refreshingly out-of-the-way and enjoyable . . . highly recommended to all comers." —*Saturday Review*

NO TEARS FOR HILDA
"It starts fine and finishes finer. I got behind on breathing watching Max get not only his man but his woman, too." —Rex Stout

THE RIDDLE OF SAMSON
"The story is an excellent one, the people are quite likable, and the writing is superior." —*Springfield Republican*

Michael Gilbert

BLOOD AND JUDGMENT
"Gilbert readers need scarcely be told that the characters all come alive at first sight, and that his surpassing talent for narration enhances any plot. . . . Don't miss." —*San Francisco Chronicle*

THE BODY OF A GIRL
"Does what a good mystery should do: open up into all kinds of ramifications, with untold menace behind the action. At the end, there is a bang-up climax, and it is a pleasure to see how skilfully Gilbert wraps everything up." —*The New York Times Book Review*

THE DANGER WITHIN
"Michael Gilbert has nicely combined some elements of the straight detective story with plenty of action, suspense, and adventure, to produce a superior thriller." —*Saturday Review*

DEATH HAS DEEP ROOTS
"Trial scenes superb; prowl along Loire vivid chase stuff; funny in right places; a fine performance throughout." —*Saturday Review*

FEAR TO TREAD
"Merits serious consideration as a work of art."
—*The New York Times*

C. W. Grafton

BEYOND A REASONABLE DOUBT
"A very ingenious tale of murder . . . a brilliant and gripping narrative."
—Jacques Barzun and Wendell Hertig Taylor

Edward Grierson

THE SECOND MAN
"One of the best trial-testimony books to have come along in quite a while." —*The New Yorker*

Cyril Hare

DEATH IS NO SPORTSMAN
"You will be thrilled because it succeeds in placing an ingenious story in a new and refreshing setting. . . . The identity of the murderer is really a surprise." —*Daily Mirror*

Cyril Hare (cont'd)

DEATH WALKS THE WOODS

"Here is a fine formal detective story, with a technically brilliant solution demanding the attention of all connoisseurs of construction."

—Anthony Boucher, *The New York Times Book Review*

AN ENGLISH MURDER

"By a long shot, the best crime story I have read for a long time. Everything is traditional, but originality does not suffer. The setting is perfect. Full marks to Mr. Hare." —*Irish Press*

TRAGEDY AT LAW

"An extremely urbane and well-written detective story."

—*The New York Times*

UNTIMELY DEATH

"The English detective story at its quiet best, meticulously underplayed, rich in perceivings of the droll human animal and ready at the last with a neat surprise which has been there all the while had we but wits to see it." —*New York Herald Tribune Book Review*

WITH A BARE BODKIN

"One of the best detective stories published for a long time."

—*The Spectator*

Robert Harling

THE ENORMOUS SHADOW

"In some ways the best spy story of the modern period. . . . The writing is terse and vivid . . . the ending full of action . . . altogether first-rate."
—Jacques Barzun and Wendell Hertig Taylor, *A Catalogue of Crime*

Matthew Head

THE CABINDA AFFAIR

"An absorbing whodunit and a distinguished novel of atmosphere."
—Anthony Boucher, *The New York Times*

MURDER AT THE FLEA CLUB

"The true delight is in Head's style, its limpid ease combined with humor and an awesome precision of phrase." —*San Francisco Chronicle*

M. V. Heberden

ENGAGED TO MURDER
"Smooth plotting."

—*The New York Times*

James Hilton

WAS IT MURDER?
"The story is well planned and well written."

—*The New York Times*

P. M. Hubbard

HIGH TIDE *(available 3/82)*
"A smooth elaboration of mounting horror and danger."

—*Library Journal*

Elspeth Huxley

THE AFRICAN POISON MURDERS
"Obscure venom, manical mutilations, deadly bush fire, thrilling climax compose major opus.... Top-flight."

—*Saturday Review of Literature*

Francis Iles

BEFORE THE FACT
"Not many 'serious' novelists have produced character studies to compare with Iles's internally terrifying portrait of the murderer in *Before the Fact,* his masterpiece and a work truly deserving the appellation of unique and beyond price."   —Howard Haycraft

MALICE AFORETHOUGHT
"It is a long time since I have read anything so good as *Malice Aforethought,* with its cynical humour, acute criminology, plausible detail and rapid movement. It makes you hug yourself with pleasure."

—H. C. Harwood, *Saturday Review*

Michael Innes

DEATH BY WATER *(available 4/82)*
"The amount of ironic social criticism and deft characterization of scenes and people would serve another author for six books."

—Jacques Barzun and Wendell Hertig Taylor

Michael Innes (cont'd)

THE LONG FAREWELL *(available 4/82)*
"A model of the deft, classic detective story, told in the most wittily diverting prose."
—*The New York Times*

Mary Kelly

THE SPOILT KILL
"Mary Kelly is a new Dorothy Sayers. . . . [An] exciting new novel."
—*Evening News*

Lange Lewis

THE BIRTHDAY MURDER
"Almost perfect in its playlike purity and delightful prose."
—Jacques Barzun and Wendell Hertig Taylor

Arthur Maling

LUCKY DEVIL
"The plot unravels at a fast clip, the writing is breezy and Maling's approach is as fresh as today's stockmarket quotes."
—*Louisville Courier Journal*

RIPOFF
"A swiftly paced story of today's big business is larded with intrigue as a Ralph Nader-type investigates an insurance scandal and is soon on the run from a hired gun and his brother. . . . Engrossing and credible."
—*Booklist*

SCHROEDER'S GAME
"As the title indicates, this Schroeder is up to something, and the unravelling of his game is a diverting and sufficiently blood-soaked entertainment."
—*The New Yorker*

Thomas Sterling

THE EVIL OF THE DAY
"Prose as witty and subtle as it is sharp and clear. . .characters unconventionally conceived and richly bodied forth . . . . In short, a novel to be treasured."
—Anthony Boucher, *The New York Times*

Julian Symons

THE BELTING INHERITANCE
"A superb whodunit in the best tradition of the detective story."
—August Derleth, *Madison Capital Times*

BLAND BEGINNING
"Mr. Symons displays a deft storytelling skill, a quiet and literate wit, a nice feeling for character, and detectival ingenuity of a high order."
—Anthony Boucher, *The New York Times*

BOGUE'S FORTUNE
"There's a touch of the old sardonic humour, and more than a touch of style."
—*The Spectator*

THE BROKEN PENNY
"The most exciting, astonishing and believable spy story to appear in years.
—Anthony Boucher, *The New York Times Book Review*

THE COLOR OF MURDER
"A singularly unostentatious and memorably brilliant detective story."
—*New York Herald Tribune Book Review*

THE 31ST OF FEBRUARY
"Nobody has painted a more gruesome picture of the advertising business since Dorothy Sayers wrote 'Murder Must Advertise', and very few people have written a more entertaining or dramatic mystery story."
—*The New Yorker*

Dorothy Stockbridge Tillet
(John Stephen Strange)

THE MAN WHO KILLED FORTESCUE
"Better than average."
—*Saturday Review of Literature*

Simon Troy

SWIFT TO ITS CLOSE
"A nicely literate British mystery . . . the atmosphere and the plot are exceptionally well wrought, the dialogue excellent."
—*Best Sellers*

Henry Wade

A DYING FALL
"One of those expert British suspense jobs . . . it crackles with undercurrents of blackmail, violent passion and murder. Topnotch in its class."
—*Time*

THE HANGING CAPTAIN
"This is a detective story for connoisseurs, for those who value clear thinking and good writing above mere ingenuity and easy thrills."
—*Times Literary Supplement*

Hillary Waugh

LAST SEEN WEARING . . .
"A brilliant tour de force."
—Julian Symons

THE MISSING MAN
"The quiet detailed police work of Chief Fred C. Fellows, Stockford, Conn., is at its best in *The Missing Man* . . . one of the Chief's toughest cases and one of the best handled."
—Anthony Boucher, *The New York Times Book Review*

Henry Kitchell Webster

WHO IS THE NEXT?
"A double murder, private-plane piloting, a neat impersonation, and a delicate courtship are adroitly combined by a writer who knows how to use the language."
—Jacques Barzun and Wendell Hertig Taylor

Anna Mary Wells

MURDERER'S CHOICE
"Good writing, ample action, and excellent character work."
—*Saturday Review of Literature*

A TALENT FOR MURDER
"The discovery of the villain is a decided shock."
—*Books*

Edward Young

THE FIFTH PASSENGER
"Clever and adroit . . . excellent thriller . . ."
—*Library Journal*

If you enjoyed this book you'll want to know about THE PERENNIAL LIBRARY MYSTERY SERIES

Nicholas Blake

☐	P 456	THE BEAST MUST DIE	$1.95
☐	P 427	THE CORPSE IN THE SNOWMAN	$1.95
☐	P 493	THE DREADFUL HOLLOW	$1.95
☐	P 397	END OF CHAPTER	$1.95
☐	P 398	HEAD OF A TRAVELER	$2.25
☐	P 419	MINUTE FOR MURDER	$1.95
☐	P 520	THE MORNING AFTER DEATH	$1.95
☐	P 521	A PENKNIFE IN MY HEART	$2.25
☐	P 531	THE PRIVATE WOUND	$2.25
☐	P 494	A QUESTION OF PROOF	$1.95
☐	P 495	THE SAD VARIETY	$2.25
☐	P 569	THERE'S TROUBLE BREWING	$2.50
☐	P 428	THOU SHELL OF DEATH	$1.95
☐	P 418	THE WHISPER IN THE GLOOM	$1.95
☐	P 399	THE WIDOW'S CRUISE	$2.25
☐	P 400	THE WORM OF DEATH	$2.25

E. C. Bentley

☐	P 440	TRENT'S LAST CASE	$2.50
☐	P 516	TRENT'S OWN CASE	$2.25

Buy them at your local bookstore or use this coupon for ordering:

Gavin Black

☐	P 473	A DRAGON FOR CHRISTMAS	$1.95
☐	P 485	THE EYES AROUND ME	$1.95
☐	P 472	YOU WANT TO DIE, JOHNNY?	$1.95

John & Emery Bonett

☐	P 554	A BANNER FOR PEGASUS	$2.50
☐	P 563	DEAD LION	$2.50

Christianna Brand

☐	P 551	GREEN FOR DANGER	$2.50
☐	P 572	TOUR DE FORCE *(available 3/82)*	$2.50

Marjorie Carleton

☐	P 559	VANISHED	$2.50

George Harmon Coxe

☐	P 527	MURDER WITH PICTURES	$2.25

Edmund Crispin

☐	P 506	BURIED FOR PLEASURE	$1.95

D. M. Devine

☐	P 558	MY BROTHER'S KILLER	$2.50

Buy them at your local bookstore or use this coupon for ordering:

HARPER & ROW, Mail Order Dept. #PMS, 10 East 53rd St., New York, N.Y. 10022.

Please send me the books I have checked above. I am enclosing $ _____ which includes a postage and handling charge of $1.00 for the first book and 25¢ for each additional book. Send check or money order. No cash or C.O.D.'s please.

Name _____

Address _____

City _____ State _____ Zip _____

Please allow 4 weeks for delivery. USA and Canada only. This offer expires 12/1/82. Please add applicable sales tax.

Kenneth Fearing

☐	P 500	THE BIG CLOCK	$1.95

Andrew Garve

☐	P 430	THE ASHES OF LODA	$1.50
☐	P 451	THE CUCKOO LINE AFFAIR	$1.95
☐	P 429	A HERO FOR LEANDA	$1.50
☐	P 449	MURDER THROUGH THE LOOKING GLASS	$1.95
☐	P 441	NO TEARS FOR HILDA	$1.95
☐	P 450	THE RIDDLE OF SAMSON	$1.95

Michael Gilbert

☐	P 446	BLOOD AND JUDGMENT	$1.95
☐	P 459	THE BODY OF A GIRL	$1.95
☐	P 448	THE DANGER WITHIN	$1.95
☐	P 447	DEATH HAS DEEP ROOTS	$1.95
☐	P 458	FEAR TO TREAD	$1.95

C. W. Grafton

☐	P 519	BEYOND A REASONABLE DOUBT	$1.95

Edward Grierson

☐	P 528	THE SECOND MAN	$2.25

Buy them at your local bookstore or use this coupon for ordering:

HARPER & ROW, Mail Order Dept. #PMS, 10 East 53rd St., New York, N.Y. 10022.

Please send me the books I have checked above. I am enclosing $ _____ which includes a postage and handling charge of $1.00 for the first book and 25¢ for each additional book. Send check or money order. No cash or C.O.D.'s please.

Name _____

Address _____

City _____ State _____ Zip _____

Please allow 4 weeks for delivery. USA and Canada only. This offer expires 12/1/82 . Please add applicable sales tax.

Cyril Hare

☐	P 555	DEATH IS NO SPORTSMAN	$2.50
☐	P 556	DEATH WALKS THE WOODS	$2.50
☐	P 455	AN ENGLISH MURDER	$1.95
☐	P 522	TRAGEDY AT LAW	$2.25
☐	P 514	UNTIMELY DEATH	$2.25
☐	P 523	WITH A BARE BODKIN	$2.25

Robert Harling

| ☐ | P 545 | THE ENORMOUS SHADOW | $2.25 |

Matthew Head

| ☐ | P 541 | THE CABINDA AFFAIR | $2.25 |
| ☐ | P 542 | MURDER AT THE FLEA CLUB | $2.25 |

M. V. Heberden

| ☐ | P 533 | ENGAGED TO MURDER | $2.25 |

James Hilton

| ☐ | P 501 | WAS IT MURDER? | $1.95 |

P. M. Hubbard

| ☐ | P 571 | HIGH TIDE *(available 3/82)* | $2.50 |

Buy them at your local bookstore or use this coupon for ordering:

Elspeth Huxley

☐ P 540 THE AFRICAN POISON MURDERS $2.25

Francis Iles

☐ P 517 BEFORE THE FACT $1.95
☐ P 532 MALICE AFORETHOUGHT $1.95

Michael Innes

☐ P 574 DEATH BY WATER *(available 4/82)* $2.50
☐ P 575 THE LONG FAREWELL *(available 4/82)* $2.50

Mary Kelly

☐ P 565 THE SPOILT KILL $2.50

Lange Lewis

☐ P 518 THE BIRTHDAY MURDER $1.95

Arthur Maling

☐ P 482 LUCKY DEVIL $1.95
☐ P 483 RIPOFF $1.95
☐ P 484 SCHROEDER'S GAME $1.95

Austin Ripley

☐ P 387 MINUTE MYSTERIES $1.95

Buy them at your local bookstore or use this coupon for ordering:

HARPER & ROW, Mail Order Dept. #PMS, 10 East 53rd St., New York, N.Y. 10022.

Please send me the books I have checked above. I am enclosing $ _____ which includes a postage and handling charge of $1.00 for the first book and 25¢ for each additional book. Send check or money order. No cash or C.O.D.'s please.

Name _____

Address _____

City _____ State _____ Zip _____

Please allow 4 weeks for delivery. USA and Canada only. This offer expires 12/1/82. Please add applicable sales tax.

Thomas Sterling

☐ P 529 THE EVIL OF THE DAY $2.25

Julian Symons

☐ P 468 THE BELTING INHERITANCE $1.95
☐ P 469 BLAND BEGINNING $1.95
☐ P 481 BOGUE'S FORTUNE $1.95
☐ P 480 THE BROKEN PENNY $1.95
☐ P 461 THE COLOR OF MURDER $1.95
☐ P 460 THE 31ST OF FEBRUARY $1.95

Dorothy Stockbridge Tillet
(John Stephen Strange)

☐ P 536 THE MAN WHO KILLED FORTESCUE $2.25

Simon Troy

☐ P 546 SWIFT TO ITS CLOSE $2.50

Henry Wade

☐ P 543 A DYING FALL $2.25
☐ P 548 THE HANGING CAPTAIN $2.25

Hillary Waugh

☐ P 552 LAST SEEN WEARING . . . $2.50
☐ P 553 THE MISSING MAN $2.50

Buy them at your local bookstore or use this coupon for ordering:

HARPER & ROW, Mail Order Dept. #PMS, 10 East 53rd St., New York, N.Y. 10022.
Please send me the books I have checked above. I am enclosing $ _____ which includes a postage and handling charge of $1.00 for the first book and 25¢ for each additional book. Send check or money order. No cash or C.O.D.'s please.

Name _____

Address _____

City _____ State _____ Zip _____

Please allow 4 weeks for delivery. USA and Canada only. This offer expires 12/1/82. Please add applicable sales tax.

Henry Kitchell Webster

☐ P 539 WHO IS THE NEXT? $2.25

Anna Mary Wells

☐ P 534 MURDERER'S CHOICE $2.25
☐ P 535 A TALENT FOR MURDER $2.25

Edward Young

☐ P 544 THE FIFTH PASSENGER $2.25

THE
ISLAND OF PEARLS

by

MARGARET ROME

HARLEQUIN BOOKS   TORONTO
WINNIPEG

Original hard cover edition published in 1973
by Mills & Boon Limited.

© Margaret Rome 1973

SBN 373-01776-6

Harlequin edition published April 1974

Printed in Canada

1776